HER COWBOY BILLIONAIRE BOYFRIEND

CHRISTMAS IN CORAL CANYON, A WHITTAKER BROTHERS NOVEL, BOOK 3

LIZ ISAACSON

feel good fiction

ELANA JOHNSON

ISBN-13: 978-1723973147

CHAPTER 1

A ndrew Whittaker cringed as the backdoor slammed shut behind him. Thankfully, there wasn't anyone around to reprimand him, but his childhood memories about not slamming the door echoed through his head.

His dad in particular had not been fond of all the loud noises, but with four boys in the house, some concessions had to be made.

The scent of warm hay and horse flesh met Andrew's nose and he took in a deep breath of it. He'd never considered himself to be a country type of person. Nor a man who could be content raising and riding horses.

But a strange sense of peace cascaded over him as he started the feeding. It was the same thing each day, and the thirteen horses that he and his brothers owned relied on Andrew to take care of them now that his younger brother, Eli, had moved to California to start a life there with his new wife.

Eli had bought most of these animals, and Andrew had *not* been happy to have them passed to him. At first. But now...now Andrew craved this early-morning animal care before he had to don the power suit and put on his public face for Springside Energy.

His older brother, Graham, was the CEO of the company, but Andrew had returned to Coral Canyon as the company's public relations director about a year and a half ago. He had the degree, and his brother needed him.

Honestly, the older Andrew got, the more he realized how much family meant to him. Especially since he couldn't seem to find someone to fall in love with and make a family of his own.

A cream and brown horse lifted his head over the door and sniffed at Andrew. "Hey, Wolfy," he said, reaching over to stroke the horse's nose. Eli liked Second to Caroline the best, but that made sense since his late wife's name had been Caroline. But Andrew had taken quite a liking to Wolfgang, and the horse always seemed happy to see him, and they'd spent a lot of hours in the mountains surrounding the lodge where Andrew now lived alone.

Well, not really.

"Bree's doin' okay," he told Wolfgang as if the horse had asked. The part-time interior decorator and gardener Graham had hired years ago had become full-time as she'd taken over Eli's responsibilities around the lodge with scheduling the horseback riding and other events at the lodge.

So much had changed in just the few weeks since Eli's wedding, with Andrew moving out of the basement and those rooms going up on the website for guests. Bree had moved into the room down the hall from Andrew, and he'd thought it might be awkward at first, with them being the only two living in the lodge now.

But it wasn't. He'd entertained an idea about asking her out for about five minutes, but there was no spark between them.

Plenty of sparks when she'd accidentally put a bowl with metal around the rim in the microwave and then grabbed it out with her bare hands.

"The bandages are almost off," he continued as he fed Wolfgang and moved down to the next stall. She still handled everything she needed to, because she could tap on a speaker icon and book groups for the theater room in the basement, or for horse-back riding birthday parties, or whatever else she did.

Andrew wasn't sure what the events at the lodge were, honestly. He spent so much time at Springside, with its building about ten miles northeast of the town of Coral Canyon, that he rarely got home before dark. Even then, he'd stop by the kitchen for whatever Celia had left for him, and stumble down the hall to his bedroom. He didn't interact with guests or deal with much else at the lodge.

"Goin' riding today?" he asked Goldie, an older horse at the end of the row. "I know you are. Make sure you edge over closer to a child." The cream-colored horse was getting up there in years, which made her calm and approachable, but she couldn't go as far as she used to.

"I'm gearing up for the unveiling of Graham's robot. October first is the big day." Not that the horses in the stable knew when October would come, but Andrew had just over three weeks to get everything in line for the huge announcement about a robot that would hopefully make Andrew's job easier. Everyone's job should be easier with the invention that would be able to detect the gasses Springside mined without having to drill.

After all, the majority of the protests he dealt with stemmed from the drilling of the Wyoming countryside. His shoulders tensed and he hadn't even put on the fancy loafers or slicked his hair to the side yet.

He unconsciously reached up and pressed his cowboy hat on his head. He much preferred the simplicity of this life, and that had surprised him the very most about Eli's departure.

He finished feeding the horses, promised them he'd be back that night, and walked back to the lodge. The scent of coffee met his nose, and he said, "Morning," to Bree as he peered into the kitchen from the mudroom. He left his cowboy boots there and went to shower.

With the suit on, every crease exactly right, and his tie the color of watermelons with a white paisley stitched into it, he slipped on the expensive loafers and stepped into the bathroom. He sprayed the gel on his hair and combed it until it was just-so. He couldn't afford to be anything but personable and professional when he left the lodge for work.

Today was no different, though the tension in his chest felt stronger than it normally did for a Wednesday. He drove the ten miles to Springside in a nondescript sedan, just like he had for months. His route took him past the front of the building, where he'd turn and park in the back, behind a coded gate.

As he eased past today, the group of people gathered there made him groan audibly. Another protest. *Great.* Just what he needed today.

Andrew eyed a woman with slightly frizzy, light brown hair. She attended every single protest, and as she walked from person to person and said something, Andrew suspected she actually organized the demonstrations.

"It's fine," he muttered to himself as he turned the corner and headed for the back lot. If they didn't bother people, they could camp on the sidewalk in this early September heat wave Wyoming was experiencing. Andrew would keep an eye on them from his air-conditioned office on the sixth floor.

His morning passed with the chants beyond his window permeating the bullet-proof glass every half an hour or so. After a while, he didn't even hear them when they started up again, as he had a difficult article to respond to and a new blog post to write about the robot.

"How's the Gasman?" Graham asked as he came into Andrew's office.

"What are you doing here?" Andrew stood and gave his brother a slap on the back.

"I'm in the basement until next week. Only a few more weeks until we reveal this thing to the whole world." Graham swallowed like he was nervous, which Andrew knew he was. Graham had spent plenty of time in Andrew's office detailing how nerve-racking it was to have something from his mind splashed on the front page of newspapers and the covers of magazines—and worse, in little headline boxes with click-bait titles below.

Andrew was used to the pressure of journalism and dealing with the media. He had a degree in journalism and public relations, and he'd literally spent his adult life writing press releases, articles, and those Internet blurbs Graham hated so much.

"How's it going down there?" Andrew leaned against his desk, wishing he could come to work in jeans, cowboy boots, and an expensive polo the way Graham did. He looked polished and professional, and everyone knew who he was, but he didn't have to wear the suit to be in the electronics lab—or the basement as he'd taken to calling it because of the cold temperatures in the room.

Funny thing was, the huge, floor-sized laboratory was on the third floor, nowhere near the basement of the building.

"It's going fine," Graham said, stepping over to the wall of windows behind Andrew's desk. "What are they mad about today?"

"It's been a while since they've been here." Andrew joined his brother. "I don't know what their problem is now." Only about thirty people had gathered on the sidewalk, and only a handful of them had signs. Weak ones too, scrawled on with thick, red permanent marker.

Red? Was that the only color in someone's purse?

He found the tall, slender woman with the frizzy hair. She'd pulled it back into a ponytail and carried a sign that read MAKE WYOMING FREE AGAIN.

He had no idea what that meant. It wasn't like the state had seceded from the Union or anything. And Springside doing the hydraulic fracturing as they extracted the gases in the rocks beneath didn't bind Wyoming or its residents in any way.

He turned away from the window just as a swell of sound rose up from the crowd. He spun back to find the majority of them swarming a woman as she walked toward the building.

"It's Mom," he said, his pulse skipping around his chest.

"Mom?" Graham asked, peering out the window, but Andrew headed for his door. The protestors could march in their circles, chant their rhymes until they went hoarse, and then pack up and go home. But they could not approach visitors to the building, nor employees. The rules had been made very clear.

"Call Security," he said to Carla, his secretary. "The protestors are approaching a guest." He skipped waiting for the elevator and practically ripped the door to the stairs off its hinges. So maybe he was a little riled up because the guest was his mother. But she'd been through enough already, and she deserved to come eat lunch with her sons without having to deal with protestors at her late husband's business.

He burst out of the lobby to a wall of heat, suddenly wishing for those arctic conditions of the Wyoming winter, which he'd cursed for the entire month of February.

"Hey," he called, drawing the attention of a few of the people on the edge of the crowd. "Step away from the guest." He strode forward with purpose, his anger barely simmering under control. He was aware that thirty people had phones and anything he said or did could be recorded, put online, and shown to the world.

A tall, black-haired man emerged from the crowd, and Andrew really didn't like that he couldn't see his mother. "Who are you?"

"You know the stipulations of the protest on our property," Andrew said. "We allow you to peaceably assemble, but you aren't allowed to interact with anyone coming in or out of the building." He tried to see past the man, but he must lift gorillas for a morning workout, because he was impossibly wide.

"Security," a man called behind him, and the crowd dispersed then. Andrew darted into them, searching for his mother. It seemed like the arrival of security had caused a panic, like his team of four men could arrest anyone. They were simply bulky like that black-haired man, meant to break up conflicts with sheer intimidation.

Someone elbowed him in their flight, and he dodged left, only to be knocked sideways by another man. "Mom?"

He thought he heard her call his name, but he still couldn't see her. Someone moved, and there she stood, a look of determined fear on her face. Andrew took two steps toward her when he got struck with a protest sign.

He tried to stay on his feet, but it was inevitable. Gravity pulled on him as pain exploded behind his right eye and down into his neck and up toward his skull. His right hand went to the injury, which meant he only had one hand to catch himself.

More pain in the knees and tailbone and wrist. Andrew honestly wasn't sure what was going on, but he knew blood dripped from his nose. He cradled his face, already imagining what the headlines would say and accompanying pictures would look like if he got photographed.

"Andrew." His mom reached him, and he grabbed onto her arm.

"Let's get inside," he said quickly, gaining his feet as fast as possible. He kept his hands up to cover his face while a security guard ushered them inside and locked the doors behind him.

"This way, sir," Neil said, and Andrew didn't question his head security detail. He followed the beefy man down a hall and into the bathroom, his best suit already ruined.

CHAPTER 2

"You just hit Andrew Whittaker," Raven said, and Rebecca Collings flinched.

"I did not."

"With your sign." Raven nodded toward the man in the expensive suit as he hurried away with the woman who had shown up. Neil, the head security guard, glanced over his shoulder and seemed to zero in right on her as if he'd be back later to take care of the situation.

Of course he would.

Becca knew the rules Springside Energy had provided. They could assemble. Chant. March.

They could not leave flyers on cars. Or use chalk on the cement. Or lipstick on the sliding glass entrance.

And they absolutely couldn't approach or speak to anyone coming in or out of the building. She wasn't even sure how the crowd had swelled and swarmed toward the woman when she'd arrived.

Becca had tried to stop them. Honest, she had.

She looked down at her protest sign as if it would have the DNA of who she'd hit. No way it could be Andrew Whittaker.

Not that she'd ever met the man, but she felt like she knew exactly what kind of man he'd be just from reading his ridiculous blog posts, Internet articles, and interviews.

And of course she'd recognize him. The guy wasn't shy in front of the camera, and just because he was the most handsome man in the entire state didn't mean what he wrote about his company was true.

"It couldn't be him." She examined the end of her sign, which was just a yardstick from her garage. Did it have a spot of blood on it? Andrew Whittaker's blood?

The man and his family owned and operated Springside, and pure mortification streamed through her.

"Ma'am." A huge man appeared at her side, making her visibly flinch and setting her pulse into an irregular rhythm. "I'm going to need the sign, and you need to come with us." He held out his hand, the black sunglasses on his face almost as dark as his skin.

With slightly shaking hands, she passed over the yardstick with a piece of poster board taped to it. So the protest had come together last minute. The quality of the signs didn't determine the worth of the message.

"Why do I need to come with you?" She glanced at the slightly smaller bodyguard behind the first man.

"We have a few questions."

They weren't cops. At least she didn't think they were. She ran her hands over her head, wishing her frizzy hair would lie as slick and flat as Raven's, who stood a few feet away. Pure anxiety flowed from the dark-haired woman who believed in the same causes Becca did.

Raven lifted her chin and stepped to Becca's side. "You can ask them here."

Sunglasses barely moved his head in Raven's direction. "You assaulted a man on our property. The authorities have been called, and I need you to come inside while we wait for them."

Becca's legs trembled, but she stayed standing. "All right." The words could barely be heard, and she started walking.

Raven jumped in front of her. "You can't go in there."

"I'll be fine," Becca said with more confidence than she felt. She eyed the building like it was a monster, with all that glass glinting down at her like sharp teeth. "I'll call you tonight."

Raven wore a look of panic, but she didn't try to stop Becca again. The air conditioning inside the building was a welcome change from the insufferable heat outside. The lobby smelled like lemonade and roses, completely unlike what she was expecting. Everything sat in its place, and she'd be hard-pressed to find a speck of dust.

The security guard led her down a hallway and through a door, with the second man behind her. She didn't like the sandwich-y feeling, but she couldn't do much about it.

"Wait here." The guard indicated a tiny ten-foot-by-ten-foot room, and Becca entered it without question. The door closed behind her, the click so final Becca felt it all the way down in her stomach.

The Whittaker's had money, and she had no idea what would happen next. As it turned out, only time passed. Becca didn't wear a watch, and she wasn't quite sure where her phone was at the moment. But it felt like quite a long time was just slipping through her fingers.

The air conditioning blew through the vents overhead, but there was no music filtering through the building—at least not in this room. She sat in a hard chair, with a small table in front of her, and nothing else.

The more seconds that passed, the more frustrated she got. Did this Andrew Whittaker think she had nothing better to do than wait for him? Surely he wouldn't come in. Maybe the police were taking his statement and then they'd come talk to her.

"Calm down," she whispered to herself, wondering if solid walls had two-way mirrors in them. This room had no windows, no mirrors, and only the door. No cameras in the corners. She could talk to herself freely.

"They can't arrest you," she said. "The Whittakers have money, but they're not cops."

She glared at the door, but it still didn't open. Did they think she just had unlimited time on her hands?

"Well, you do," she said to herself. She'd finished up her freelance consultation with the State Wildlife Division, and she didn't have anything else lined up yet. Thus, the impromptu protest this morning. At least it got her out of the house, right?

Still, sitting in this silent room was a form of torture Becca never wanted to experience again. Her impatience swirled through her, driving her emotions toward the breaking point.

So when the door opened, Becca jumped to her feet. "It's about time," she said to the men entering. "You know you can't just keep me here."

The two security guards came in and took positions in the corner of the room, allowing space for another man to enter.

Andrew Whittaker.

Becca sucked in a breath that tightened her chest. Her heart zinged around inside her chest at the nearness of him.

He exuded power from his shoulders though the suit had been replaced with a black polo that stretched nicely across his chest. Maybe she'd had to wait for him to drive home and change his clothes.

Or his driver, because Andrew Whittaker didn't seem like the kind of man who did anything without an entourage.

She cut a quick glance to his security detail, a flash of pride at her assessment striking her bloodstream and giving her some confidence.

"The door wasn't locked." Andrew gestured to her chair. "Please, sit." He spoke in an even tone, perfectly political and polite. Professional all the way to the very last cell of his body. This was the Andrew Whittaker he allowed other people to see, and Becca squinted at him, wondering if she could get close enough to him to find out the real dirt.

She gave herself a little shake, hiding it by stepping over to the chair she'd burst out of. She sat and folded her arms, her insides quaking and this the only way she knew how to keep herself from saying or doing something she'd regret later.

Andrew exhaled as he sat too, and Becca couldn't see any evidence of his injury. "I'm sorry," she blurted anyway, immediately wishing her mouth would just stay shut. Apologizing was practically an admission of guilt, like she knew she'd done something wrong and needed to make it right.

Andrew cocked his head slightly. "For what?"

She cut a glance at the security guard standing a few feet from her. "I...don't know?" Now that she looked at him a little closer, his nose looked a little puffy, and he definitely had a skin-colored bandage on his right temple. Maybe she'd had to wait so long so someone could dye the bandage to match his skin.

He gazed at her evenly, which she found absolutely unnerving. Somehow, she managed to stare right back. She might not have his millions. Or his finesse. In fact, she wanted to reach up and smooth down the frizz she knew stuck up from her scalp. But she'd gnaw off her own hand before she'd allow herself to do that.

"Are you going to arrest me?" she asked, lifting her chin. If he didn't have such beautiful eyes—green with a lot of brown in there—it wouldn't be so easy to look right at him.

Andrew did the strangest thing—he tipped his head back and laughed.

Confusion raced through Becca at the speed of sound. And it brought with it all the wonderful undertones of his laughter, infusing into her soul and making her want to be alone with him while they walked down the street, or maybe into the theater, him laughing at something brilliantly witty that she'd said. Then he'd kiss her and they'd get in a fancy limousine.

She startled at the strange, fantastical paths her thoughts had just taken.

"No," Andrew said, around a mouthful of chuckles. He sobered and looked right at her again. Past all her defenses. Past the protest signs and the prickly personality. "I'm here to offer you a job."

CHAPTER 3

"I'm sorry. What?" Rebecca Collings' wore confusion in the cutest way, something Andrew had tried to dismiss a half-dozen times already.

"I need an assistant," he said. "Well, not really an assistant." His gaze flickered to Isaiah, the huge security guard who'd helped Andrew get himself and his mother to the safety of the building. Graham had taken her to lunch already, back in town, leaving Andrew to deal with the protestors, as usual.

Didn't matter. Andrew was exceptionally skilled at handling difficult situations, and besides, he really did need an assistant.

"A what, then?" Rebecca asked, still with her arms clenched across her chest.

"I think I'm getting ahead of myself," he said. "I'm Andrew Whittaker. I run all the media operations for Springside."

"I know who you are." And she didn't seem particularly impressed, not that he expected her to be.

"And you are?" he prompted in the kindest voice possible.

"Oh, uh." She glanced at the security detail too. "I'm Rebecca Collings. I go by Becca." She pressed her eyes closed as if she'd given away national secrets by revealing her name.

"Becca," he said with a smile. "I think you hit me with your yardstick."

"It was an accident." She leaned forward, her light blue eyes earnest and intense. "I told everyone to stay put when that woman arrived," she insisted. "I know the rules."

"Of course you do," he said. "I think you come here at least once a month, don't you?"

"No," she said, but Andrew thought so. There was never a protest here without her. "The last one was in July."

"Oh, so you missed August."

Anger flashed in those eyes that seemed to pull on Andrew no matter how strongly he wished they wouldn't. He didn't understand this sparking sensation in his bloodstream. He let go of the schedule of protests and said, "That woman was my mother."

Horror marched across her face. "I'm so sorry. I promise I told the group we can't approach people."

"I believe you," Andrew murmured, and he did. He drew in a big breath and centered his thoughts again. "I would like to offer you a job. It's not a protesting one, though, and your checks would have Springside Energy on them."

Interest entered her expression now, and Andrew put a small, placid smile on his face. Nothing for her to read into. Nothing for her to deduce.

"What's the job?"

"We're going to be announcing something very soon, and I need a press secretary."

"I read about your big announcement on your blog."

Andrew couldn't help feeling impressed. "You read the blog?" He seriously didn't think anyone but him and his mother read those entries.

"Most of what you write is pure drivel," she said, realizing a half-beat too late what she'd said. "I mean...I just think it's like you're trying to sprinkle rainbows and unicorns on what you really do here."

Andrew tilted his head, his patience with this woman growing thinner by the moment. He'd taken plenty of time to change his clothes, get cleaned up and bandaged, and look up everything he could about Rebecca Collings.

He knew she had two degrees: one in environmental studies and one in public policy. He knew her last job with the State of Wyoming had ended thirteen days ago. He knew she was born and raised in a town called Newton, with a population of only six hundred and thirty-four. She'd gone to college at the University of Wyoming in Laramie, and she now lived in Coral Canyon.

"What do you think we really do here?" he asked.

She looked less sure of herself then. "You drill with the hope of finding your precious gas, when you don't even know if it's there."

He couldn't really argue with that. "We have ways of knowing where to drill."

"They're not good enough," she shot back.

"Well, they're about to get better." This woman made something fire inside him that hadn't gone off in years. "That's why I need you. We'll be doing several events around the state, and I need a pretty face and the brains behind it so I'm not the only one talking."

There. He'd said it. Becca did possess a beauty that Andrew hadn't seen in a while, and with the right makeup, a haircut, and some perfectly tailored clothes, everyone would listen to exactly what she said.

He'd been thinking about hiring a press secretary for months, but his schedule hadn't allowed it. But now, it seemed the stars had aligned, and this woman knew a lot about him and Springside already. Maybe what she thought she knew wasn't all rainbows and unicorns, as she'd said, but he'd save a lot of time if she said yes.

"There is no way I'm working for you or this company," she said, standing up. "And if I'm not under arrest, I'm leaving."

Andrew waved at the closed door, his heart sinking to the soles of his second-best pair of shoes. "You're not under arrest."

"Great. Good-bye, Mister Whittaker." Becca stepped over to the door and practically ripped the knob off as she yanked it open.

Andrew listened to the sound of her angry footsteps as they moved down the hall. He sighed and turned to Isaiah and Tom. "I need to talk to Dwight. Do we know if he's in today? Or out on a drill?"

"I'll find out." Isaiah stepped out of the room, grunting as he did. A scuffle followed, drawing Andrew's attention.

Isaiah had bumped into someone, and he said, "Excuse me, ma'am," as they completed their dance and he moved further into the hall to reveal Becca standing in the doorway.

"How long will the job be?" she asked, her tone high on the demanding scale.

Andrew stood, hope lifting his spirits so high he couldn't stay seated. Please, he prayed. Not only was Becca perfect for the job because of her past antagonism for Springside Energy, she was a woman Andrew wanted to spend more time with, get to know, maybe....

He let his thoughts die there. If he hired her, dating her would be inappropriate.

His heart warred with the desire coiling through him. "Indefinite," he said. "Springside constantly has a barrage of media needs."

"And the pay?" She cocked her hip, and though she wore jeans and a forest green T-shirt with a white pine tree in the middle of it, Andrew found her downright attractive.

Attraction. That was this electric feeling zipping through him. What had been sparking in him for an hour now.

"Name your salary," he said. "I'll pay it."

Surprise bolted across her face, and Andrew needed a thread to keep them connected. If she walked out now, he'd have to employ tactics to find out where she lived or her phone number.

"Why don't you give me your phone number?" he said, as if it were a question. "And you can take some time to think about it. Text me your demands." He added a smile to the statement so she wouldn't think he found her demanding. "I would need an answer fairly quickly. Perhaps by the weekend?"

"That's fine."

"Great. You can leave your number with Stephanie at the front desk."

She glanced left and right, both ways down the hall.

"She should be in the lobby," Andrew said. "I'll get it from her when I'm finished here."

Becca nodded, a bit of uncertainty still hanging in her eyes. She turned and left without a word, and Isaiah stuck his head back into the tiny room. "Dwight is on a drill. He'll be here tomorrow."

Andrew stepped over to the doorway and watched Becca Collings stride with those long, long legs into the lobby. "I don't think I'm going to need to talk to him," he said with a smile. "She's going to take the job."

"You think so?" Isaiah sounded doubtful. "She's got a lot of emotion inside her," he said. "And she hates Springside."

"Which is why we need her," Andrew said, echoing what he'd already told Graham. The people in Coral Canyon and the other towns where Springside did their hydraulic fracturing were sick of his face. Sick of his rhetoric. Sick of the company coming in and disrupting their way of life, though Andrew didn't think his face or the things he said were really the problem. And the fracturing didn't disrupt their way of life all that much. No, they simply didn't like change. Didn't like that Wyoming wasn't the wilderness it used to be.

Graham's robot would change a lot about their process, and it was a much more accurate system than the scans they did now. He needed someone at his side. And that someone couldn't be better than Becca Collings, a woman who'd long spoken out against Springside and everything they meant and did.

He clapped Isaiah on his beefy shoulder. "Is it time for lunch?"

The man laughed, and together with Tom, they went over to the cafeteria. Andrew kept a silent prayer going in his mind that Becca would accept his offer of employment. If there was one thing his parents had taught him, it was the power of prayer.

No, his prayers didn't always come true, or turn out the way he'd like. But that didn't stop him from making sure the Lord knew what he wanted and why.

———

HE'D JUST PULLED INTO THE PARKING LOT IN FRONT OF THE LODGE when his phone buzzed. He sighed, the sun already making its way behind the huge Grand Teton Mountains and casting the valley where Coral Canyon and Whiskey Mountain Lodge sat in navy shadows.

Couldn't work wait for thirty minutes? He'd honestly left his office *thirty minutes* ago. What could have possibly happened?

But it wasn't from anyone at work. Or one of his brothers. Nor his mother.

But an unknown number, from the state of Wyoming. He could deduce that from the area code. He tapped to open the message and read aloud, "Hey, this is Becca Collings. I want to talk a bit more about the job. When are you available?"

His stomach growled, reminding him that the lunch he'd eaten in the cafeteria had been hours ago, and the calories from his afternoon protein bar were long gone.

Right now, he typed out. *Have you eaten dinner?*

He could get into town in twenty minutes, meet her anywhere she wanted. The fact that he was so keen to do exactly that wasn't lost on him. And he knew it would be more than a casual business meal. At least for him.

I could eat, she responded.

How about Lonestar? The steakhouse had big, cushy booths,

perfect for feeling like the conversation was private. Plus, he liked the ribeye there, and no one made better mashed potatoes. His mouth watered just thinking about it. *Twenty minutes?*

He put the car in reverse and backed out of the space before she answered. Even if she said no, he now had Lonestar steaks in his mind, and he wanted to get one in his mouth. He brought the car to a stop before pulling onto the road.

Or I can come pick you up, he typed, regretting that he'd already asked her to meet him.

I can meet you there. Twenty minutes.

Andrew nodded though there was no one to communicate with, and got going. He wouldn't pick up business associates, and this better stay business until he had her on the payroll. *Even then....* he thought, though his heart danced at the opportunity to go out with Becca, even if it was business.

He just hadn't been on a date in a while. Or even been excited about a woman he'd met. He didn't get much opportunity to play the single scene, and that had always been just fine with him. But it meant most of his dates came from women he met at church, and well, none of them had made his heartbeat ripple the way Becca had.

He pushed the thoughts of a relationship with the woman out of his mind. He needed a press secretary, and she was absolutely the perfect person for the job. He couldn't mess things up with that just to see if she'd let him hold her hand.

CHAPTER 4

B ecca stood on her back patio, her phone still bright in her
hand. She couldn't believe how her day had gone. This
morning, if someone had told her that she'd be going to dinner
with Andrew Whittaker that night, she'd have laughed in their
face.

But she was totally going to meet Andrew Whittaker for
dinner in twenty minutes. Well, fifteen now, if she could get
herself away from the eight pet food bowls on the back patio.

She'd already filled them for the strays she fed and watered.
She didn't see the dogs and cats much, but they ate the food she
left out so she knew they were around. Inside, Otto, her yellow
Lab, was also scarfing down his dinner. He lived in the house,
and she'd raised him from a puppy. All the other animals
stopped by when they needed a bite to eat, and she finally
turned away from her yard and went inside.

Otto looked up from the bowl where she'd scraped the
scrambled egg and hot dog hash she'd made for him. So she
cooked meals for her dog. Big deal. She wanted him to be happy
and healthy, and it gave her something to do with her time.

The microwave beeped at her, reminding her that she'd put
in a frozen burrito before texting Andrew about needing to talk.

She opened the door and closed it again so the appliance would stop beeping and hurried into her bedroom.

She couldn't go to dinner at a steakhouse with the handsomest man in town wearing jeans and a dirty T-shirt. Though he'd already seen her in this outfit, it simply wasn't good enough for someone like him.

After changing into a pair of black slacks and a white blouse with tiny palm trees on it, she considered her footwear. She didn't own heels, as she already stood five-foot-nine-inches tall. So a pair of black sandals would have to do.

She tried to tame her hair, but it had been allowed to be in its frizzy element all day, and it didn't care about steakhouses or billionaire bachelors.

Becca paused, still looking into her own eyes. "You don't care about steakhouses or billionaire bachelors either," she told herself, hearing the lie between the last three words.

Of course she did. She had a mortgage, a car payment, and dozens of stray animals to feed. She hadn't worked in almost two weeks, and here Andrew was, offering her whatever she wanted.

Name your salary, he'd said.

I'll pay it, he'd said.

But could she really work for Springside Energy?

Her phone screen brightened again, drawing her attention away from her makeup-less face. She swiped it open when she saw Raven's name. *How did things go? You never called.*

Becca jammed her thumb on the call button at the top of the text message. She hadn't called, because she'd been in a bit of a stupor since leaving Springside hours ago.

"Hey," Raven said. "Are you okay? You're not in jail, are you?"

Becca tried for a light laugh, but she'd never been great at hiding how she felt. "No, I'm not in jail. Everything went fine."

"So...you bloodied up Andrew Whittaker and they let you go?"

Becca moved into her bedroom and collapsed onto her bed. She'd be late for the steakhouse, but she needed some advice. "Not only that," she said. "But he offered me a job."

"What?" Raven's shriek almost broke Becca's eardrum. She quickly explained the situation, then told her best friend about the date that she was supposed to be on in five minutes.

"I mean, it's not a date," she said. "It's a business meeting." She exhaled, needing to get the terms straight before she left the house. "How can I take a job there?"

"You need a job," Raven said carefully. "Maybe you can influence what Springside does—or doesn't do—from the inside. I mean, do you really think that company does anything before Andrew knows about it? Gives it his okay?"

Becca shook her head and ran her hand down Otto's back as he walked in front of her. "He's not the CEO. He doesn't make the decisions."

"You can bet he's involved in every one," Raven said. "He'd have to be. He has to be prepared for all press requests and questions, any media fallout…he definitely has his finger on the pulse of that company."

Becca ground her teeth together and looked up at the ceiling. "I think you're probably right."

"Just see what he says. Tell him you need some huge amount of money. See what he says. Maybe he'll be like, 'Nope. See ya.'" Raven laughed, and Becca joined in. But she'd seen Andrew's face when he'd said *Name your salary. I'll pay it.*

And she knew Springside could not only afford whatever she named for a salary, but that he would definitely pay it. The real problem was knowing whether she could handle working for this company she'd opposed for so long.

Influence what Springside does—or doesn't do—from the inside.

"I better go," she finally said. "I'm late already."

"Call me as soon as you get home," Raven said. "Don't forget, or I'll call you in the middle of the night!"

Becca groaned, as she really liked her sleep, and promised she'd call Raven after dinner.

"And there's another problem," Becca muttered to herself. "You have a crush on the gorgeous billionaire who runs the company you've opposed for a decade."

———

BECCA SAT IN HER CAR, UNABLE TO GO INSIDE THE STEAKHOUSE. SHE was twenty minutes late now, and Andrew hadn't texted yet. Why couldn't she go inside?

Someone knocked on her window, causing her to yelp and flinch away from the glass. Her heart bobbed in the back of her throat in the few moments it took to identify Andrew's face. He gestured for her to get out of her car, and she complied.

"I'm starving," he said. "If you're not going to come in, can we drive through somewhere?" He didn't seem upset or bothered that she hadn't been on time. He wore the same slacks and black polo from earlier that day, and he tucked his hands in his pockets while he waited for her answer.

"I'll come in," she finally said, and he grinned. That action on his face should be illegal, as it made her pulse jump around like it was at a dance party.

"Great," he said. "Because they have the best food here." He waited for her to step and then he fell in line beside her. "I may or may not have already eaten a plate of the bacon ranch cheddar fries...."

Becca couldn't help the laugh as it burst from her mouth. "So you must really be starving."

"I am," he insisted as he took a double-step in front of her and held the door open to the steakhouse. "They were serving fettucini Alfredo in the cafeteria today, and it didn't even have chicken."

"Oh, so you're the meat and potatoes type, are you?" She

paused just inside the door, the noise from the steakhouse meeting her ears.

"About," he said. "My brother's wife has a cattle ranch, so we eat a lot of beef." He shrugged and signaled to the hostess, who took them back immediately even though there were several others obviously waiting. "I like it. Tastes good."

He led her to a booth in the corner, away from most of the noisier customers. "Thanks, Jo," he said as if he knew the hostess personally, which he probably did. Everything about Andrew was sheer perfection, right down to how he waited for Becca to slide into the booth first before he sat opposite of her.

"See? Remnants of my fries." He grinned again, and Becca's stomach swooped for every other reason other than that she was hungry. "I did order water for you. Figured that was safe."

She put her hands flat on the menu. "What would you order for me here?"

A light entered Andrew's eyes that hadn't been there before, and Becca really liked it. Her flirtatious question had obviously hit its mark, and she wondered if she should be happy about that, or scared out of her mind.

"You seem like the pasta type of woman," he said. "But I'd still get you the...." He cocked his head, something he did a lot, and said, "Braised short ribs, with a baked potato, not mashed, and the vegetable medley—no, a side salad. With ranch dressing."

Becca blinked once before laughing again. "All right, sir. Let's go with that."

"Did I get it right?" he asked, hope shining in his face.

"Pretty dang close." She would've made her baked potato "wild," which meant they'd stuff it with cheese, bacon, and green onions.

The waitress arrived before she could tell him that, and he ordered the ribeye with mashed potatoes for himself and exactly what he'd predicted for her.

"And make my baked potato wild," she added, giving him a *Nice try* look.

He chuckled as the waitress moved away, lifted his water to his lips, and as he set his glass down said, "Okay. So tell me what we need to talk about."

So he wasn't going to waste any of the meal on small talk. Becca liked that, while at the same time, she didn't.

"I'm still thinking about the job," she said.

He nodded, his attention fully on her. She could tell he was smart just from the edge in his eyes. But she'd read his writing, so she already knew that. Seen his pictures in papers, magazines, and the Internet.

"I want benefits too," she said. "If the job is really indefinite."

"It is," he confirmed as if she'd asked. "Springside is only growing, and I can't keep up by myself anymore. How my father did this without a public relations manager, I'll never know."

"Your father—" Becca cut herself off, as she didn't need to speak ill of the dead. And besides, this was Andrew's father. She couldn't say anything cruel about him.

Andrew had heard something in those two words though, because he turned stony.

"Your father did the best he could," Becca amended. "But he wasn't great with the community or the press. Not the way you are."

Andrew softened a little, but not nearly to as pliable as he'd been a few seconds ago. "I've done the best I could." He sighed and glanced out of the booth, toward the rest of the restaurant. "It's never enough, though, I'll tell you that." He gave her a weary smile that opened the door to what his life might really be like. And it wasn't all designer suits and perfectly styled hair.

"Which is why I need you," he said.

Becca noted that he didn't say "someone like you." She tried not to let the words warm her, but they did anyway, all the way from her toes to her nose.

"Okay," she said. "So benefits. I need to know a little bit more about the hours."

"Oh, the hours are insane," he said. "The morning isn't too bad. Come in at nine or ten or whenever. But once you're there, I swear the building finds things for you to do."

"Is that why you're wearing the same clothes from earlier?"

"I had just gotten home when you texted. Didn't even go inside." He took another drink, something else behind those words. Becca couldn't even imagine what.

"It's almost eight-thirty now." And she'd kept him waiting.

"Yep." He met her eyes. "The hours are insane. And we'll be traveling for the entire month of October. I don't know what your family situation is like, or if you have pets or children or whatever."

Becca thought his face colored slightly, but she couldn't be sure in this dim light.

He cleared his throat. "And you still need to name the salary."

"I don't have children," she said. "Not married. No boyfriend in town. Or family for that matter." Saying it out loud sounded pathetic. What did she have in her life?

"I do have a giant yellow Lab. I'll have to figure something out for him."

Andrew nodded. "Any boyfriends out of town?"

Becca blinked rapidly, realizing she'd said *No boyfriends in town* like she might have one somewhere else. The very idea was laughable. But Andrew simply stared straight at her, waiting, expectant. He showed zero emotion on his face, and Becca didn't like that she couldn't get a read on him.

She especially didn't like the storm swirling through her. "No," she said, her voice one click down on the emotional scale. "No boyfriends out of town either."

"Ah." Andrew nodded again.

"What about you? Your girlfriend is okay with you hiring a woman and traveling with her for a month?" Two could play his game, and Becca felt sure she would've known had Andrew Whittaker started dating someone. The gossip mill in Coral Canyon was alive and well, after all.

"Oh, all the women in my life are happy I'll be gone," he said with that sexy grin. "Celia won't have to make dinner, and Bree can doctor up the coffee how she likes."

"Celia and Bree?"

"Our chef and event planner at Whiskey Mountain Lodge." Andrew gave her a smile, seemingly at complete ease across the booth.

"Do you live at the lodge?" she asked.

"Yes."

Becca wasn't sure what to do with the information. "I heard they were renting it out again. Parties, horseback riding, corporate events, or just to stay the night."

"All true," he said, and nothing more.

"And you own it."

"Well, my brother bought it. But yes, the Whittakers own it."

"What do you do there?"

"I take care of all the horses."

Of course he did, as if he knew a cowboy was a siren's call to Becca's heart and soul. *Dear God,* she prayed. *How am I to resist him now? Should I even be resisting him?*

The waitress arrived with their food, and Andrew lit up like a little boy on Christmas morning.

A feeling of peace flowed over Becca, and all of her uncertainties disappeared. She liked Andrew, and accepting this job meant she could spend a lot of time with him. No, she didn't particularly like Springside Energy or what they did, but she could enact change from the inside.

She picked up her phone while he picked up his fork. She typed out a number and sent it to him. Three feet away, his device buzzed and he looked at it. "You texted me?" He glanced at her and swiped his phone open.

"You can't see your texts without opening them?"

"I like it that way," he said. "I just need to know who's texting. I generally already know what they're going to say."

She made a grab for his phone before he could tap on her message. He dropped it in surprise, his eyes glinting with amusement as he scrambled to pick up his phone. "What are you doing?"

"If you generally know what people are going to say, what did I say?"

He studied her for a moment, something hot and pulsing passing between them. He had to feel that, but he gave no indication that he could.

"I honestly don't know," he said. "You're sitting right there. So…maybe that you want the job? Maybe you don't want to say it out loud?"

"Oh, I want the job," she said, feeling bolder and braver than she had in years. Ever since Jarom had told her it was too difficult to be with someone as smart and intimidating as she was. That remark had cut her legs out from under her, and she'd spent a while wondering what was wrong with being smart.

"So then that text is what you want me to pay you." He nodded toward the phone, a smugness in the set of his mouth.

She found him…annoying. Handing the phone back, she said, "You think you're something, don't you, Mister Whittaker?"

He opened his phone, tapped, and read her text while she dressed her salad. His laughter made her look up.

"It's a deal, Miss Collings. I'll get the paperwork ready by tomorrow afternoon, and you can stop by at your earliest convenience."

Becca nodded and tucked into her food, her thoughts tumbling at what she'd just done. She didn't believe Andrew did anything on someone else's convenience schedule, so she'd get a time from him before the night ended.

She had three weeks to figure out what to do with Otto, not to mention all the strays. Oh, but she wasn't going to mention any of them to Andrew. He, as her employer, didn't need to know about her obsession with making sure the abandoned animals of Coral Canyon got fed. The last thing she needed was for him to label her a crazy cat lady, whether it was true or not.

"Okay," he said. "With the business out of the way, tell me what you like to do for fun." He cut his steak into precise pieces and swooped up a bite of mashed potato with it.

Becca didn't know how to answer. With the business done, was this a date? Her heart crashed against her ribs, desperately hoping so.

"Why does it matter?" she asked.

"Because we have a lot of free time while we drive from place to place," he said. "Might as well know how to fill it."

That didn't really give her an answer as to whether this was a date or not, but at least she'd dressed up. "I like reading," she said, thinking that a perfectly safe answer.

CHAPTER 5

Andrew thoroughly enjoyed dinner with Becca. So much that the thought of her sitting across from him and the floral scent of her perfume stuck in his nose kept him awake.

He couldn't believe she'd taken the job. Gratitude filled his heart, which also kept him from falling asleep. And hey, if she worked for the company, he suspected there'd be a lot less protesting going on too.

He did wake in the morning, which meant he had fallen asleep at some point. Bree was already in the kitchen, the coffee already made, and Celia was there too, stirring something on the stove.

"Morning, ladies," he said as he reached for a mug in the cupboard.

"You're up late today," Bree said.

"I guess." Andrew poured his coffee and added a lot of sugar to it. "Had a late business dinner last night." He hadn't really gotten home late, and he didn't really like the classification he'd just given to the dinner. But he supposed it was all true.

"Oh?" Celia asked, glancing up from her pot. "What are you working on now?"

"I hired a press secretary." He grinned, because he really did need help with the public relations at Springside.

"Who is it?" Celia asked. "I thought you said this town didn't have qualified people for that."

"I was wrong."

Bree sucked in a breath and then laughed. "I've never heard a Whittaker man say they were wrong."

"Whatever," Andrew said, rolling his eyes. "I don't go around acting like I know everything."

"No," Celia said with a smile. "You simply do know everything."

"Oh, that's just not true." He didn't like this conversation and he had thirteen horses to feed that morning. "I'll be in the stables."

"Wait," Celia said. "Who did you hire?"

"A woman named Rebecca Collings?" He glanced from Celia to Bree, noting the shock on both of their faces.

"Becca Collings?" Bree repeated. "The woman who hates anyone who even so much as goes off the trail on a hike?"

Surely she wasn't that bad. "Yes," he said simply. "She's coming to sign the paperwork this afternoon." He needed to call Carla before he went out to the stables, so she could get the employment packet ready for Becca.

"Wow," Bree said, and Celia added, "I'm sure she'll be fine."

Andrew paused in his escape toward the mudroom. "Why wouldn't she be fine?"

"No reason." But Celia definitely had reasons. Andrew didn't care. He liked Becca, and the woman was qualified in more ways than one to be his press secretary. He reminded himself that he needed someone with her perspective and point of view to win over communities and point out things he simply didn't see because of his position in the company.

So he put on his cowboy boots and left the lodge, the door slamming closed behind him. This time, he didn't even care.

He stomped about halfway to the stables before he calmed

down, and by the time he pushed into the barn to feed the horses, he'd settled back into his public relations director skin, any personal frustration and problems concealed where no one could see.

Not that it mattered out here, and he exhaled roughly. "Hey, guys," he said to the horses. "So I couldn't come last night. You got fed, right?"

Laney had a hired hand who worked for her, and Andrew had been using him more and more, and already signed him to do all the feeding during the month of the tour. Andrew didn't want to give up his morning ritual quite yet, so he opened outside doors and let the horses into the corral so he could clean out stalls.

He'd pasture the horses today, and call Jake and ask him to get them back inside that night. Because Andrew was hoping for another date with Becca, even if he had to make it a business meeting.

He wondered if he could be brave enough to ask her to dinner outright. Call it a date.

"A date," he said under his breath, the words a little tricky coming out of his mouth while he was alone in the barn. Wolfgang huffed, and Andrew looked up from the corner where he'd been pitching new straw.

"A date," he said to the horse. "Can you believe it? I went on a sort of date last night." I mean, he didn't hold her hand. Or ask her out again. But they'd had a good conversation about the job, and he'd learned a few things about what she liked to do in her spare time.

"Reading," he listed off to the horse. "And she has a dog. She likes to ski in the winter. And Wolfy, she likes bacon and cheese on her potatoes." It didn't matter that nearly the entire population liked bacon and cheese on potatoes. It was something they had in common and Andrew was seizing onto anything he could. Because he knew she didn't like Springside Energy, and had spent years disliking him too.

She hadn't said that directly, but it was a vibe Andrew had picked up on. He'd learned to trust those feelings over the years, and he was determined to win over Becca Collings. He didn't believe that the attraction he felt to her was one-sided, especially the way she'd lingered near her car after their meal.

"Oh my heck," he said, the words exploding from his mouth. "I should've asked her out again last night." He looked at the horse, but Wolfgang didn't confirm or deny. "I've already messed up."

He finished the stall and pulled out his phone, dialing Graham. His brother often drove his step-daughter to school and then went to the office, if he was coming in that day.

"Hey," Graham asked. "Give me two seconds." He obviously moved the phone away from his mouth, but Andrew still heard, "All right, Bay. Have a good day. Wait, wait, wait. Don't forget this."

Scuffling and static, and then the slamming of a car door, and Graham returned. "All right. What's up?"

"I would like to talk all the way to the end."

"Oh, boy," Graham said. "Lay out the rules."

"No laughing. I am *way* out of my element here, and I already feel stupid." He wandered out of the stable and around the side of it toward the corral and pastures. The horses seemed perfectly happy out here, and Andrew turned the handle on the spigot so he could fill the outdoor troughs.

"I agree to the stipulations of this conversation," Graham said dryly.

"Great," Andrew said, thinking of how hot it would get that day. Maybe he should have Bree come check on the horses that afternoon. "So I hired a press secretary yesterday."

"Becca said yes?"

"I said I would like to talk to the end."

Graham grunted, so Andrew continued with, "It took some convincing, but seeing as how she doesn't have a job, I was right in thinking she'd be pretty desperate." He had told Graham that yesterday, when Graham had argued against the idea of offering the job to one of their loudest protestors.

"So we went to dinner last night," Andrew said, setting the hose in the long trough along the back of the stable. "And it was great." Andrew sighed as he looked into the blue, blue sky. "And I…she stood by her car when it was over, like she didn't want to get in, and then she finally did and drove away. I should've asked her out then, right?"

"Let me rephrase," Graham said. "You went to dinner with our new press secretary, like a date? And then didn't ask her out again when she clearly lingered before leaving. And you're wondering if you've messed something up with her on a personal level."

"About that, yeah," Andrew said, not really liking the gruffness in his older brother's tone.

"I think you messed up about the time you went to dinner with an employee."

"She wasn't an employee at the time, and we don't have an official policy on co-workers dating." Andrew would know, as it was his job to make sure anything that was media-worthy about the company was controlled, contained, and kept quiet.

"You're the boss," Graham said.

"I like her," Andrew said simply. "She's the first person to even stir anything in me in years."

"She hates our company."

"She said yes to the job." Andrew felt like he was arguing with a brick wall. And he really didn't like that Graham wasn't happy for him that he'd found someone whose company he enjoyed enough to spend more than ten minutes with.

"I think if you start something with her, it should stay on the down-low until the tour is over, at least," Graham said.

"Should I call her now and ask her out?"

"Are you going to see her today?"

"Yes. She's coming to sign paperwork this afternoon."

"Ask her before she signs," Graham said. "Then you can claim the relationship started *before* she began at Springside."

It wouldn't be a lie. Andrew had felt fireworks the moment he'd sat across from her in that tiny room on the first floor.

"And Andrew?" Graham asked.

"Yeah?"

"I hope it works out with her."

"Thanks." Andrew hung up, a smile drifting across his face despite the amount of work he still had to do in the stables—and at Springside.

He had time for one more text, at least. *How about lunch at Springside today?* he sent to Becca. *I can show you our top-notch cafeteria. You get a free meal for every shift you work. I think lunch today is French dip.*

She didn't answer until he'd finished with the horses, showered, and knotted his blue and black checkered tie with extreme precision.

Trying to seduce me with roast beef?

Andrew couldn't help the laugh that spilled from his mouth. *Is it working?*

I'm not sure beef is entirely convenient for me today.

Andrew really liked her wit, and he chuckled again.

"What's so funny?"

He glanced up at Celia, who set a stack of toast in front of him and asked, "Scrambled eggs?"

"Yes, please." Graham's words about keeping things secret between him and Becca ran through his mind on a constant loop. "Just a funny text," he said, hoping Celia would buy the little fib. She didn't seem to care who he texted and turned to crack eggs into a bowl.

Yes, I think it is. Noon okay? Becca's text made his palm buzz the same way his pulse currently was.

Andrew thought of how busy the cafeteria would be at noon. Plenty of people to see them, see her. But of course they'd see her. She was the new press secretary, and soon enough, she'd know everything he did about Springside, its policies and its people.

Besides, if the cafeteria was too busy, he could take her on a tour of the building before they ate.

Noon's great, he sent and tucked into his breakfast, more happiness coursing through him than he knew existed.

Hopefully, with a bit of prayer and luck, Becca would be able to see him as a separate entity from the energy company. After all, she didn't *know* him, so how could she hate him?

CHAPTER 6

Becca stroked Otto's head absently, wondering what she should wear to eat lunch in an office cafeteria. She sincerely hoped the food and atmosphere was better than the school cafeterias she'd eaten in.

Did she have time to go to the salon and get her hair treated? Straightened?

She shook her head. Andrew had already seen her with the frizzy mass of curls, with no makeup on her face, and in those jeans....

But she'd definitely need a new wardrobe to be a press secretary. She made a mental note to ask him for the budget for new clothes during their lunch. Then it was a working lunch and not a date. Right?

Honestly, she really needed a classification for it, because she'd slept about four hours last night trying to put labels on everything that had happened that day.

She left the big window overlooking the backyard and went into her closet. She had a black pencil skirt she wore to church, and she threw that on the bed. She could wear the sandals, though a press secretary should wear heels. She also owned a pale pink blouse her mother had sent her for her last birthday, and it looked professional with a simple gold chain around her neck and a bit of smoothing gel in her hair.

The curls still seemed out of control to her, but she embraced them, swished a bit of mascara on her eyelashes and left with just enough time to arrive at Springside by noon.

This time, she didn't sit in the car and let her worry eat at her. She got out and strode toward the building she'd only been inside once.

Stephanie, a lovely brunette probably a decade older than her, smiled and lifted onto her feet. "Becca. I wasn't expecting you until later." She picked up the phone. "Let me call up to Mister Whittaker's office.

"He's supposed—"

"I'm here," Andrew said, entering the lobby from one of the hallways. He wore a navy blue suit that looked like it had been made especially for his frame. Nothing pulled too tight. Nothing was too loose. Not a strand of his hair sat out of place, and those delicious eyes devoured her as he walked closer.

"Oh, Mister Whittaker." Stephanie replaced the phone in its cradle.

"She's taking a tour," he told her. "Carla's got the paperwork almost finished." Andrew leaned against the reception counter. "I'm sorry I didn't warn you she'd be coming early." He switched his gaze back to Becca, and heat traveled through her whole body. "You ready?" He swept his arm around the lobby as if that was the whole tour.

Becca didn't know what to say, so she just nodded, smiled at Stephanie, and let Andrew lead her away from the other woman.

"I'm taking a tour?" she whispered to him when they were out of earshot.

"Mm," he said noncommittally—which annoyed her greatly. He opened a door to a room with a window at the back of the lobby. "Can we talk in here for a minute?" He looked casual and cool, but there was something in the undercurrent of his voice.

"Sure," she said brightly and entered the room first. This

room was four times as large as the one she'd waited in yesterday, with a long, oval table surrounded by cushioned office
chairs.

She didn't sit but turned to face Andrew as he followed her
inside and closed the door behind her. He wouldn't look straight
at her, another huge red flag.

"What's going on?" she asked, maybe a little too demanding.

He cleared his throat, and it was actually refreshing to see
that he wasn't infallible. "Okay, I'm just going to say this."

"All right."

But he said nothing. He shifted his feet. Adjusted his tie like
it was choking him. He made her nervous too.

"Just say it," she said, fearing he'd offered her the job prema-
turely and was now going to take it back. Thus, he'd invented a
tour so he could get her into this sterile room and break the bad
news in person. At least he was enough of a gentleman to do
that.

But she'd literally never seen him shift or appear uncomfort-
able, ever. And she'd seen plenty of interviews and pictures of
the man.

"I'd like to ask you to dinner tonight." His words rushed out
of his mouth. "As a date. A date, with you and me. Me and you
on a date." He clamped his mouth shut as redness crept from
under his collar and settled in his cheeks.

Pure joy filled Becca. All kinds of spluttering things filled her
head too, but she managed to say, "I'd like that," without
making herself into a fool.

That beautiful grin exploded across Andrew's face. "Okay,
great. We really can take a tour, if you'd like. Or we can go check
the lines in the cafeteria." He flinched toward her like he'd touch
her, maybe hold her hand as they sauntered through the Springside Energy building.

"Is lunch a date too?" she asked, desperate for those labels.

Andrew took a long moment to shake his head. "No, so we
probably should talk about a couple of things."

"What things?" Maybe Becca should've taken a seat, but she hadn't known this would be a long, serious conversation.

"My brother thinks it might come off as...inappropriate if it's public knowledge that we're, uh...." He cleared his throat. "Dating."

Understanding hit Becca. "Because you're my boss."

"I'm not your boss," he said.

"You're everyone's boss." She grinned at him. "Right?"

"I'm *Andrew*." He patted his chest a couple of times. "Not Graham. Graham's the boss."

"Which is why our relationship has to be secret." She cocked her hip, enjoying this a little too much. Just the possibility of a relationship was thrilling to Becca. She'd all but given up on finding someone who could appreciate her intelligence, her quirkiness, and her less-than-Hollywood appearance.

"It was Graham's idea, yes." Andrew leaned against the edge of the conference table. "But to be clear, I think he's right. We don't want anyone to accuse Springside of anything unethical."

"Is it unethical for us to, you know. Date." She could barely say the word, and sudden appreciation for how hard Andrew had worked hit her.

"No," he said. "We don't have any company policies against co-workers dating. Besides, you don't even work here yet."

"Oh, so you asked me out before I signed the paperwork, is that it?"

Andrew's smile reached all the way into those beautiful eyes. "You don't miss much, do you?"

"No," she said. "And don't forget that."

"I'm actually counting on it," he said, reaching for the door. "So while we're at work, or anywhere people can see us, we'll be co-workers. Not...together. So lunch today is a work meeting."

"Good," she said, though she wished it were a date. "Because I have more questions."

"Okay," Andrew said, completely unruffled. "And I was

right about the French dip. They're also serving a Cobb salad today, if you'd prefer that."

Becca said, "I'll decide when we get there," and let him lead her out of the conference room. She did love a Cobb salad, but she was feeling particularly like beef today, and she was only slightly ashamed to admit that it was because of the tall, strong man beside her.

She let her hand brush his, and he pulled away and put a step of distance between them. Humiliation dove through her, and she regretted her actions. He'd literally just said that they would be purely professional at work.

Becca liked the professional Andrew, but she really wanted to see what he looked like with a cowboy hat on, maybe his jeans a little dirty. Heck, she'd take just seeing him in anything but a suit.

She smelled the French dip before the cafeteria came into view, and her taste buds made the decision for her.

"So," he said as they joined the line, which wasn't too terribly long. "What questions did you come up with?"

"It's about my clothes," she said, indicating the pale pink blouse. "This is literally the nicest thing I own. Unless you want me behind a microphone in a Greenpeace T-shirt, I'm going to need a new wardrobe." She took the tray he handed to her. "I'm wondering if there's a budget for that."

"Sure," he said. "I can get you a card today. Or we have accounts at both department stores in town."

"And I what? Saunter in and say, 'Put this on Andrew Whittaker's account.'" She looked at him and found him blinking back at her. "Oh, wow. That *is* what I would do."

"If I've called and authorized you to purchase clothes, yes. Otherwise, they'd call me while someone brought you a bottle of water."

Becca shook her head, charmed and yet annoyed at how efficient everything within Springside was. And she knew who to attribute that to—the man right beside her.

She fought against the strong tether pulling her toward him. It seemed ridiculous in the first place. She'd literally spent *years* disliking this company, what they did and what they stood for, and every man who ran it. How had Andrew charmed her so completely in less than twenty-four hours?

She thought of a sermon she'd often reflected on. One from many years ago, when she was fresh out of college and just starting her adult life. The pastor had warned against making quick judgments, for they almost always proved to be wrong in some way.

Could she have been wrong about Springside and the Whittakers all this time? If so, maybe she and Andrew really did have a chance at a relationship.

But if not…Becca didn't want to consider the consequences of risking her livelihood, her future, and her heart to Andrew, even if he was the most handsome and perfectly polished man on the planet.

———

The next day, Becca twisted and turned in front of three full-length mirrors, Raven smashed into the fitting room with her. "What do you think?"

"I think it's too bright," Raven said immediately. "You've never looked good in yellow. Makes your skin look washed out and it competes with your hair."

At least Raven was honest. Becca valued that above almost anything, and she nodded. "You're right."

"You look better in cool colors like blues, purples, and greens. Pink too."

"But the slacks are nice, right?" She turned and lifted the bottom of the shirt to see her rear end.

"Very nice. You should get those."

They were a simple pair of black slacks, but the material felt twice as thick as anything Becca currently owned, and the price tag made her gasp.

"You're not paying," Raven said, wiggling her fingers for Becca to step out of the pants and hand them to her.

Becca complied and took the skirt Raven handed to her next. "This one's too lacy."

"Just try it with the sweater."

Becca didn't want to think about a time when she'd need a sweater, as the heat wave that had hit Wyoming was determined to stay for a few more days. But she shimmied into the dark, eggplant-colored pencil skirt that had thick white lace all over it.

It fit great, and made her feel very feminine. She didn't normally dress in skirts except for Sundays, but her new job would require it whenever she stepped foot outside the house. She wasn't fussy enough for this job, but she was determined to do the best she could. And if that meant wearing a lacy pencil skirt, she'd do it.

She slipped her arms through the pale blue tank top and covered it with a matching cardigan before turning to the mirror.

Her breath stuck in her chest. She barely recognized herself in these clothes. And with makeup and heels and her hair hanging in loose waves around her face? She'd absolutely be the press secretary Andrew needed.

"See?" Raven said, standing to pull on the sweater in the back. "This is my favorite thing you've put on. Is it heavy?"

"The skirt is a bit. But it could be cold in October."

"And you'll still have the job in January, right?" Raven's eyes met Becca's in the mirror. Becca wanted to spill everything about her dinner date with Andrew the night before, but she'd agreed to keep the relationship a secret, and that meant from best friends too.

"Right," she said. "So what else?"

"The black dress with gold flowers."

"I don't like it."

"I get one thing for free." Raven grinned as she picked up the silky dress and took it carefully off the hanger. "Just put it on, and then decide."

"Fine." Becca complied, but the bust fell in all the wrong ways. "It's too big."

"Yep. Not good. Take it off and then let's go get lunch." Raven reached for the door handle and slipped out of the dressing room.

Becca shook her head and changed back into her own clothes. She'd gotten quite a few things in the few hours they'd been in the store, and she spoke briefly with the saleswoman about coming back to get them after lunch. The woman was all smiles and *yes ma'ams*, and Becca decided she could really get used to being treated like a princess.

At the same time, her stomach soured. She'd never been motivated by money, though she could admit having it made life easier.

"So," Raven said, hooking her arm through Becca's as they walked past the makeup counter. "Something's going on you haven't told me."

"No," Becca said quickly. Maybe a little too quickly.

"You sure?" Raven asked.

"It's just the new job," Becca said. "It's stressful. He wants me to be perfect. Look perfect. Talk perfectly. I might only last a week there."

"Have you learned anything about this big project they're unveiling?"

"Not yet." Andrew hadn't even brought it up once, and Becca had forgotten about it as well.

"Well, I can't wait to hear all about it." Raven steered them toward a fast casual restaurant with the best fried chicken in four states, and Becca replaced her worry over what the energy company could have up their sleeve—as well as how she could hide a relationship from Raven—with honey mustard and seasoned potato wedges.

It actually worked for the first few bites too. Then the reality of going to work at Springside Energy on Monday morning hit her with the strength of an avalanche.

CHAPTER 7

Andrew lightly touched his temple, examining the mark there. It was small, barely noticeable, but his mind whirred around Becca and how he'd come to have her in his life.

"The Lord works in mysterious ways," he said to his reflection. He rarely went to work on Sundays, instead choosing to catch a ride with Graham, Laney, and Bailey as they went down to town for church.

His phone bleeped, signaling that Graham had just left the ranch a mile down the road, and Andrew swept his device into his pocket and headed for the hallway.

Bree passed just as he opened his door, and they nearly collided. "Going to church?" she asked as she stutter-stepped ahead of him.

"Yes," he said, noticing her long, flowery dress. "You?"

"Obviously." She gave him a smile and ducked into the office.

"Graham will be here any second."

"I know. I'm grabbing something for him."

Andrew continued toward the front door, opening it just as Graham arrived in his brand new minivan. Andrew snorted, the sight of his tall, broad, cowboy-hat-wearing brother behind the wheel of a minivan too comical to ignore.

Graham glared at him through the windshield, and Andrew kept on laughing.

The window rolled down, and Graham growled, "Not a word."

"I don't think I can ride in this thing," he said, looking into the back, where the kids sat.

"We don't all fit in the SUV. Not if Bree comes too." Graham cut a glance toward the front door, and Bree came running out.

"I don't think I can fit in the back," Andrew said. He had his suits tailored to his exact measurements, and climbing into a minivan wasn't on his list of activities. The seams would surely rip if he tried to maneuver into the back of this vehicle.

"I'll get in the back," Bree said, already opening the door and folding herself onto the bench seat in the way back.

"We put Bailey back there too," Laney said. "So you can ride right there by the door."

Andrew eyed the seat and figured it was just like riding in the front. At least he had a tinted window, because showing up at church in a minivan? That wasn't going to help his reputation.

He got in and grinned at baby Ronnie while Graham did a wide U-turn to get them back out of the parking lot. "How are things going with Becca?" he asked.

Andrew seized. Had his own brother just outed him? "What do you mean?" he asked, carefully, looking into the rear-view mirror to meet his brother's eyes.

"She started last week, right? How do you think she'll do as the press secretary?"

Andrew's pulse quieted, but the adrenaline didn't fade as quickly. "Oh, no. She hasn't started yet. She signed paperwork on Thursday. Went shopping for a new wardrobe over the weekend. She starts tomorrow."

"New wardrobe?"

"She's going to be a very public figure," Andrew said, a note of defensiveness in his voice. "She has to look the part."

"And she didn't have clothes?"

"She has a T-shirt that says 'Grow a tree.' You want her to wear that while we tour the state to talk about your robot?"

"No," Graham barked.

"Look, don't be mad at me that you're driving a minivan." Andrew grinned at the growl coming from his brother, and he looked at his sister-in-law. She tried to hide a smile, but she didn't quite pull it off and ended up emitting a laugh before she could cover her mouth.

"What? You think he's funny?"

"Maybe if you didn't wear the hat." Laney reached over as if she'd touch Graham's hat, but he planted one palm right on top of his head.

"I am *not* driving this thing without it," he said darkly. "It's the only thing preserving my manhood right now."

Laney laughed fully then, and Andrew joined in. "The van is necessary," Laney said. "It's your family's fault." She threw a playful glance at Andrew, clearly enjoying teasing her husband.

"I can drive myself to church," Andrew said.

"I said I would drive," Laney said. She turned back to Andrew. "He wouldn't let me."

"Da-da-da-da," Ronnie babbled, and Laney said, "You tell him, bud. Should've let me drive."

Andrew laughed—everyone did, except Graham, which somehow made everything funnier.

THE NEXT MORNING, THERE WASN'T MUCH TO LAUGH ABOUT. BECCA was due to arrive any moment, and Andrew's nerves fired like cannons. Sunday had been nice, with a great sermon, a picnic at Laney's house, and then a long horseback ride through the woods that bordered the lodge.

Everything about Monday was the opposite. He had a meeting with Beau that morning, as his youngest brother was the company's legal counsel. He also had to suffer through an hour or two with the accountant to get approval for the new wardrobe and then the tour costs. After that, he'd meet with Dwight to go over the final reveal plans. He hoped he had time to eat. Oh, and train Becca in her new job.

All while trying to pretend he didn't like her for more than a co-worker. But he'd been thinking about her since their dinner a few nights ago, and they got along quite well through texting.

He wasn't great at that though, so the chats were short, with long periods of time in between. He simply didn't like the medium for real conversations, though he had learned that she did not like clam chowder or raisins during one of their message streams.

So he rushed through his morning chores, showered, and showed up at Springside forty minutes before he normally did.

"She's in her office," Carla said, a look of worry in her brown eyes.

"Who is?" Andrew took the slips of paper his secretary handed him, scanning the messages. She'd tried emailing or texting him who had called or what the news was, but Andrew had missed too much that way. He much preferred just stopping to talk with her, have her explain some of her shortened scribbles, and then tackling the biggest items first.

"Becca Collings," Carla said, rising from her seat. "She got here twenty minutes ago, and I didn't really know what to have her do. I texted you."

Andrew's heart ba-bumped in his chest and rose to his neck. "I was probably driving," he managed to say. "Thanks, Carla."

"That bottom one is from Dwayne," she said as he walked past her desk toward his office. "He needs to reschedule."

"I'll talk to him first then." Andrew lifted the fistful of slips above his head in his traditional *thank you, Carla. You're the best* wave, and glanced to his right. An empty room had once sat there, but he'd had a custodian and Carla make it into an office for Becca last Friday. A new desk, a comfortable chair, a computer, and a telephone, and she was ready to move in.

He went into his office though every cell in his body screamed at him to go into hers. He'd call over to Dwayne first. Make sure he had his paperwork ready for both Beau and Paul, the accountant, and then he'd go see how Becca had settled in.

Andrew took a moment to admire the Wyoming landscape from his windows, then he sat.

"Morning."

"Oh." He flinched and jerked, his chair sliding backward. "You scared me."

Becca stood in front of him, wearing a dress that screamed professional and yet highlighted all her best features too. She seemed taller, and as he stood, he could see her heeled feet.

"Nice dress," he said, his voice only slightly strangled. But wow, his tie had never felt like it was cutting off his air before.

She swished the hem of it, sending the flowers on the cream-colored fabric moving. "Thanks." She sat in the chair across from him. "I don't know what I'm supposed to be working on."

"Did you get logged in to your computer okay?" He resisted the urge to look over her shoulder and out toward Carla. Of course it made sense to have Becca in his office. And of course she wouldn't know what to do unless he told her.

"Yes, there was a pristine pink Post-it note all ready for me." She smiled, and he noticed the shiny pink gloss on her lips. He stared, perhaps for a moment past comfortable, because she cleared her throat and added, "Carla said you had a few meetings today. I was hoping I could sit in on them. Start to learn what you do, so I'll know what I should do."

Andrew blinked, feeling like the biggest fool on the planet. "Yes, yes," he said. "Beau should be here in ten minutes, and then we have to go to the fifth floor and meet with the accounting department. Dwight cancelled." He sorted through the slips of paper and found the one with Dwight's name on it.

"Well, I'm about to cancel with him. Then we can go over the unveiling. That will be your first task." He leaned his elbows on his desk, glad for the physical barrier between them, because he had such a strong desire to take her into his arms and kiss her right there.

And Andrew didn't know what to do with those feelings. So he stuffed them deep, deep, and hoped that boring business meetings would beat the attraction right out of him.

"The unveiling?"

"Yes, I'll need you to sign these." He opened a drawer, but the paperwork wasn't there. "Carla?" He got up and went to the doorway. "I need the non-disclosure docs about the robot for Becca to sign."

"Yes, sir."

Andrew cringed. Carla was at least a decade older than Andrew, and he'd never asked her to call him sir. In fact, she rarely did. Why had she now?

He returned to his desk with, "Carla's printing them."

"Non-disclosure?" Becca asked.

Andrew looked at her, finding interest and doubt in her eyes at the same time. "My brother has invented a robot," he said carefully, as she hadn't signed the paperwork yet. "That's what we're unveiling. Nothing's been done with it yet."

She narrowed her eyes, her mouth tightening. "What do you mean? It's not ready?"

"No." He shook his head, wishing his thoughts would align as perfectly as the creases in his slacks. "The robot is ready. Nothing for the press or media has been prepared. We have a plan for the unveiling. We have stops scheduled. Meetings with mayors and then town halls. But for the next three weeks, you'll be learning everything you can about our company, the history, what we do, and how this robot will change it for the better."

He watched her, as he'd never really given her a job description before. Her shoulders squared and she lifted her chin, a move he'd seen her do several times. It was her way of showing her determination, of not backing down from whatever was in front of her. It was incredibly sexy, that two-inch motion of her chin, and Andrew smothered his smile.

"Then you'll be preparing our speeches, the media releases, the magazine articles. You'll coordinate with all the mayor's offices in the towns we'll be visiting, all the newspapers no matter how small, and making sure every photo from every photographer is approved before it goes to print, either digitally or physically."

Her eyes widened now and her mouth opened slightly. Andrew did chuckle then. "I told you it was an insane job."

She snapped her lips together, her eyes blazing with fire now. "I just have one question."

"Oh, I doubt that." He leaned back in his chair and steepled his fingers together. "You have a million questions, Becca. It's something I rather like about you."

That stunned her into silence for a few beats, then she said, "What were you planning to do if I said no to this job?"

"I knew you wouldn't say no."

"You have never advertised this job. What if I didn't hit you with my yardstick? Had you even been looking for a press secretary?" She leaned forward too, and Andrew couldn't escape from the sharpness of her gaze.

"I'd been thinking about it for a few months," he admitted. "But no, we hadn't been officially looking."

"So what would you have done if I'd said no?"

He sighed, almost rolling his eyes but catching himself at the last moment. He did not let his nerves show in public. Or his frustration. Never anger. And never did he make someone feel like he didn't appreciate every single thing they said.

"Becca," he said calmly. "I would've done whatever it took to be ready for this tour if you had turned down the job."

Whatever it took. That was the motto for Andrew's life. And he knew what that meant for something of this magnitude. It meant he wouldn't have slept. He'd have hired Laney's cowhand to take care of the horses full-time. He'd have skipped church. Heck, he'd probably have set up a cot in what was now Becca's office and slept there so he could get everything done that needed to be done.

"But you did say yes," he said as Carla appeared in the doorway, a few sheets of paper in her hand. She paused, never entering when he was meeting with someone without his permission. "And I'm going to have Carla pull a few files for you on our company, just as soon as you sign this non-disclosure form." He gestured for Carla to come on in.

She did, and set the papers on the desk in front of Becca, along with a black pen.

"Then we'll do our meetings," he spoke as if sitting in a meeting was akin to going to the beach. "And then, I'll show you our robot."

He noticed her extreme interest at that, and she reached over and picked up the pen. She signed her name with a flourish, and Andrew nodded at Carla. The secretary swept the papers away and he said, "Get her everything, Carla. And let me know when Beau shows up, would you?"

Everyone stood, and Carla led the way out of his office. He buttoned his jacket as he followed the women out, and he paused at Carla's desk. "I'll be in Graham's office for a few minutes."

He walked away without waiting for her confirmation, because he really needed a space that wasn't perfumed with the sweet smell of Becca Collings.

Graham, unsurprisingly, was not in yet, and Andrew closed the door and leaned against it, breathing deeply.

"How am I going to keep things professional?" he whispered to the ceiling, hoping his words would make it all the way to God's ears. "I can't even get through a ten-minute conversation with the woman without wanting to kiss her."

Andrew imagined God to be laughing at him, because he'd never not known what to do in a situation. But with Becca he felt like he'd broken both arms and was trying to figure out how to write with his feet.

CHAPTER 8

Carla was nothing if not efficient, and it didn't take her more than ten minutes to knock lightly on Becca's open door, a thumb drive pinched in her fingers. "This has everything you need," she said with a smile.

She took a few steps and slid the thumb drive across Becca's desk. "I'll let you know when Beau arrives. I believe Mister Whittaker wants you in on the meetings today."

"Thank you," Becca said. "Oh, Carla," she added when the woman started to leave. "Where do I start?"

"I numbered them for you." She gave a quick smile and left Becca with the thumb drive containing everything about Springside Energy.

Everything.

A wicked thought entered her mind. So she'd signed that non-disclosure form. What could they really do if she took this thumb drive and published it on the Internet?

"Probably prison," she muttered. She hadn't actually read the non-disclosure agreement, but she knew Andrew and his brothers would have every T crossed and every I dotted. Their brother the lawyer had probably drawn up the agreement and all the contracts she'd signed last week to be iron-clad.

And surprisingly, she didn't want to destroy Springside Energy. Her heart had really started firing when Andrew had mentioned a robot, and she wasn't fundamentally against mining. She just didn't like how exploratory the fracturing had to be to find the gas.

But a robot...if it could detect the gas *before* any hydraulic drilling....

She pushed all her speculations away and plugged in the thumb drive. Her computer was state-of-the art, and an icon popped up on her screen in less than two seconds. She double-clicked it and at least two dozen files sprang into a box. Twenty-seven to be exact, as Carla had indeed numbered them.

The first file bore the label of *The Whittaker Family*.

Becca wasn't sure if she should be surprised or disgusted at the egotism. She paused and thought about Andrew. Yes, he had every single stitch of clothing in the exact right spot. Not a hair on his head sat out of place. Even his beard was perfect.

But he didn't seem to carry the arrogance she'd assumed he would. So maybe she'd made a few assumptions about him and his brothers—*and his father?* her mind whispered.

It was really the senior Whittaker that Becca had a problem with. She double-clicked the file, even more surprised when a family tree popped up instead of a plain text document like she'd been expecting.

The four boys sat at the bottom, neatly labeled in a serif font. She hovered over the oldest, Graham, and found a few sentences about him, including his birthdate, graduation dates, degrees, and his position in the company. A picture with a mom, dad, and child showed in the corner and she clicked on that.

A box covered most of the tree and detailed Graham's more personal life. He was married to Laney, and they had one child, Ronald. Bailey was his step-daughter, and he suffered from mild asthma.

The files were extremely thorough, and she learned that Andrew had once broken his leg while waterskiing, and that he'd gotten his tonsils out when he was seven years old. He'd never been married and had no kids, so his personal file was quite sparse. She knew everything in the professional bio already, as it was common knowledge for someone so public.

Eli had been married to a woman named Caroline, but she'd passed away over five years ago. He'd recently gotten married to Meg, and they lived in California with Eli's son Stockton.

Beau had never been married, had no kids, and in fact had never left Coral Canyon for longer than it took to graduate from college. He'd done that in Wyoming too, and Becca felt a kinship for the youngest Whittaker brother whom she'd never met. He felt like a lifelong lover of Wyoming, same as her.

The telephone on her desk beeped, startling her while she moved the mouse to learn more about Andrew's parents. "Mister Whittaker is ready for you, ma'am. If you'll come out, I'll show you to the conference room."

The phone beeped again, and Becca stared at it. This job was so different from anything she'd ever done before. Number one, she'd never been called ma'am. Were thirty-seven-year-olds even old enough to be called that?

Number two, while she'd been to plenty of meetings, none of them happened in conference rooms. Big, open spaces while people yelled at each other, sure. Or a tiny office in the back rooms at the State Capitol, yes.

But Carla led her down the hall and around a corner to an immaculate conference room, complete with a projector mounted on the ceiling, a huge screen and whiteboard, and another wall of windows.

A man who obviously came from the same family as Andrew turned from those windows, and he too wore a suit and tie. The difference was the cowboy hat and the cowboy boots.

Becca smiled at Beau and said, "You must be Andrew's brother," as she went around the table to shake his hand.

"That I am," he drawled, obviously ten times as country as Andrew. "You must be our new press secretary."

She extended her hand. "I'm Becca."

"Beau." His smile was genuine, crinkling the corners of his eyes and filling his whole face.

"Oh, good." Andrew bustled into the room carrying an armful of folders. "You've met Beau." He closed the door behind him and took a seat in the nearest chair. "Paul apparently double-booked, so we have about forty-five minutes before we need to be in his office."

He started sending folders down the table, though neither Becca nor Beau had taken seats yet.

"Sit, sit," he said. "Let's start with the blue one. Beau, that's for you. It's Becca's new file. I want copies here in our usual places, and one at your office."

Beau picked it up but didn't open it. He sat at the corner of the table, still near the windows. "I can come later."

"We won't have time." Andrew glanced up and went right back to the list in front of him. "Becca, you'll need a red one and an orange one." He flipped open the red, apparently deciding to go in the order of the colors of the rainbow.

"This is our permission form and packet. Anyone we talk to has to sign it. It gives us permission to use their name and picture however we see fit, and ensures that they have to get our permission before any quotes or pictures are released. You'll need a lot of copies of these. Beau, anything specific she needs to know about these or can she look through them and get the gist?"

Beau took several long seconds to answer, and Becca could tell that it drove Andrew one rung higher on his frustration level. He kept his face placid, as if he had all the time in the world for his brother to speak. But Becca could see something brewing right beneath his skin. She'd felt it in his office too.

"I think she can get the gist," Beau said. "I really can come another time."

Andrew blinked at him. "The orange one is new documentation I need you to review, edit, or whatever so we're in compliance with the laws regarding public safety."

Becca perked up at that. She was well-versed in public safety. "I can do that," she said.

"You don't have time." Andrew didn't even look at her. "Beau can do it. He usually does."

"I have a degree in public policy," she said, unsure as to why she was arguing to put more work on her plate. But why wouldn't he even look at her? She felt her own frustration rise, and she worked to be as cool and collected as the great Andrew Whittaker always was.

"I need you to go over the trademark registrations," he continued, pushing a thick packet toward Beau. "It has to be done by the end of the week so the SonarBot and all its related technology, past, present, or future, can't be stolen. The list of what needs to be protected is in there."

Beau stacked the packet on top of the folders without looking at it. "Are you okay, Andrew?" He peered at his brother like there was something seriously wrong with him.

"I'm fine." He checked a box on his paper, but Becca didn't think he was fine. She exchanged a glance with Beau, and he lifted one shoulder in a shrug. She immediately deemed him a gentle giant and wondered why she'd judged him so quickly. She hadn't even known who he was.

But thanks to the family tree, she knew he'd been engaged once but his bride-to-be had called the wedding off the night before the nuptials. She also knew he'd had to take the entrance exam to law school three times before he made it in, but that he was a brilliant lawyer and had never lost a case. Never.

Andrew said something else, but Becca didn't hear him. Beau started talking too, and she let them carry on their meeting. Andrew didn't slide her any more folders, nor say her name, and when he stood, she did too.

"Thanks for coming, Beau. Tell Mom I'll try to make it to dinner this weekend, okay?"

"Oh, she's not doing dinner this weekend."

Becca paused, pretending to straighten the already straight papers inside her folder. Andrew and Beau stood in the doorway, though, and she couldn't leave them to this private conversation.

"Why not? She does a Saturday night dinner every weekend." Andrew and Beau were the same height, and if they tried to walk through the door together, they wouldn't be able to because of the width of their shoulders.

"She has a date." Beau really popped on the T-sound on the word date.

"What?" Andrew's disbelief filled the whole room. "A *date*? With who?"

"Admiral Church."

"Admiral Church?" Andrew's eyes searched his brother's. "And she said yes to that guy?"

"He's a good guy," Beau said.

"Why is this okay with you?" Andrew moved out of the room, and Beau went with him.

"Why is it *not* okay with you?" Beau countered, such a lawyerly move that Becca smiled.

"Dad's been dead for two years, Beau. And she's dating already?"

"Almost three," Beau said, saying something else that got lost as they rounded the corner and left Becca standing in the doorway of the conference room.

She wasn't sure why, but her heart felt a bit hollow. She'd known that Ronald Whittaker had died suddenly over the holidays almost three years ago. "Maybe you've never thought of him as someone's father. Someone's husband," she whispered to herself. She clutched the folders in her hand until her fingers hurt, thinking how she would feel if her father passed away that evening.

Not only that, but Andrew had barely spoken to her during that meeting. She had more paperwork to read and he'd denied her the opportunity to work on the public safety document.

Carla appeared at the end of the hall. "There you are." She gestured for Becca to come. "Andrew is looking for you. You're supposed to be headed up to the fifth floor for the accounting meeting."

Becca walked forward, her new heels rubbing along the tops of her feet uncomfortably. "Sorry," she said.

"Oh, don't apologize." Carla pointed to the elevator. "He took the stairs. I swear, that man can't hold still for longer than five seconds. Fifth floor. Ask for Paul Wilmington."

"Paul Wilmington," Becca repeated. She stepped over to the elevator and pushed the call button, her emotions simmering in a very bad way.

By the time she arrived on the accounting floor, she was ready to give Andrew a piece of her mind. He waited on a sofa in the lobby, looking at his phone, and she marched over to him.

"You couldn't have waited thirty seconds?" she demanded.

He looked up, and he wore a mask. A horrible, stony mask that revealed nothing of what he was thinking or feeling. "I didn't want to be late."

"You knew where I was. Took Carla two seconds to send me up here." In fact, he would've had to walk right in front of her to get to the stairs. "And, in case you haven't noticed, you're not late." She folded her arms and glared at him.

He glanced around the lobby, but Becca didn't care who heard their little spat. "Sit down," he said quietly.

Becca didn't want to comply, but her shoes really should've been broken in before wearing them for a full day of work. At the very least, she should've brought an alternate pair of footwear should these not work out.

She sat, but refused to rub her feet or act like anything was wrong at all. "And in the future, Mister Whittaker, I'd appreciate eye contact during a meeting when you're speaking to me."

Finally, a hint of emotion touched his expression. Was it sorrow? Regret? Something else? "Noted."

"What was with that?"

"I'm trying really hard here," he said under his breath, his mouth not moving at all.

"Trying to do what?"

"Andrew?" The secretary stood. "Paul's ready for you."

Andrew didn't answer her question. He stood, buttoned his jacket, and said, "Thank you, Jeannie. Have you met our new press secretary?" He slipped easily behind his public relations persona, flashing that charming smile, and Becca put on her game face too. "This is Becca Collings."

"Nice to meet you," she said, wondering how many more times she'd say it that day and if she could do so without choking on the words.

CHAPTER 9

Andrew sat in his office, the door closed and the lights off. He needed to apologize to Becca, but he couldn't bring himself to go next door and say the words.

He flipped his phone over and over, wondering if a texted *I'm sorry* was lame. It was in his world, but he loved the written word so maybe it was okay.

She'd want more than an apology too. She'd want an explanation. And while Andrew had one, he didn't necessarily want to tell her why he'd acted like a beast during both meetings that morning.

He'd seen her leave for lunch with Carla ten minutes ago, and he knew his secretary would be back in twenty-five. No more, no less. She was as regimented as he was.

Then he and Becca would be going over to the basement to meet Graham and the SonarBot.

"Better do it before then," he muttered to himself, tapping out the apology on his phone.

I'm sorry. I'm trying to figure out how to be around you at work.

Was that enough of an explanation? Would she understand what he meant? Did it give away too much of the stormy emotions inside him?

He wasn't sure, and he was tired of thinking about it. So he sent the message and got up from his desk. If he didn't go down to the cafeteria and eat, his next meal would be at dinner that night.

He opened his door and headed for the elevators, needing the sanctuary of the small space for a few seconds. The cafeteria buzzed with chatter and laughter, and he grabbed a premade sandwich and a bag of chips. The cashier, a woman named Ava-Jane, smiled at him and wrote his name in a book. He could actually eat as much as he wanted, but he tried to never go over his allotted one meal per shift, same as anyone else.

He scanned the cafeteria and found Becca eating with Carla and another secretary from another part of the building. Her back was to him, so he took a few moments to simply watch her. She really was perfect for this job, and he hoped he hadn't messed things up too badly between them.

Upstairs, he ate in his quiet office, proud of himself when Carla and Becca returned exactly when he thought they would. Carla settled at her desk, but Becca came right into his office and closed the door.

"I got your text," she said, her voice a bit quieter than he thought normal.

"I am sorry."

She sat across from him and crossed her legs, the motion so distracting, Andrew forgot how to breathe. "Maybe this isn't going to work out."

His eyes flew to hers. "What do you mean?"

"I mean, maybe this job isn't right for me."

"Of course it is." She couldn't quit. "You'll be brilliant at this job."

"Can I ask you a question?"

Andrew smiled. "Becca, I want you to ask me a million questions. It's actually one of the reasons I wanted you. For the job," he added quickly. "You're a thinker. You're going to make me think about what I think."

She squinted, the doubt plain to see. "This is not a job-related question."

"Oh." He licked his lips, wishing he had a mint to take away the vinegary taste in his mouth from the chips. "All right."

"Do you really think we can work together and have a secret relationship?"

"I—yes," he said. "I just need to figure a few things out."

"Like how to look at me during a meeting."

"Apparently." He had tried to avoid making eye contact, because his mind went a bit blank when he looked directly at Becca. And he couldn't control what emotion would display on his face. He hadn't wanted Beau to see anything, but his brother had known something was off anyway.

"And how to listen to me when I talk."

"I do listen when you talk," he said.

"I should be doing that public safety review," she said. "Why does Beau need to do that?"

"Because, Becca, once you see this unveiling plan and the SonarBot, you're going to be neck-deep in reports, articles, phone calls, logistics, and travel details."

"We're working together on those, right?"

"Yes, but I still have other things to do to prepare for the tour."

She nodded, though she clearly hadn't said everything she wanted to. "So, let's get to it then. Are we doing the unveiling plan first, or am I seeing the robot?"

"Are you mad at me?" he asked, feeling weak and not understanding why he needed her reassurance.

"I'm...adjusting," she said.

"I told you our relationship would have to be undercover."

"I know." She lifted that chin. "But I guess I thought you could still act like a human in public, and just be my boyfriend in private."

Boyfriend.

Is that what I am? he thought but didn't dare articulate. They hadn't even kissed yet. And he'd held her hand for a few minutes after dinner the other night.

"I can act like a human," he said.

"Good," she said. "I want to see the robot first, and that means you've got to take me down where your brother is."

"Graham knows about us."

"Does he now?" A dangerous glint entered Becca's eyes.

"Becca," he said in a warning voice, and she laughed. "What?" he asked.

"Can you please relax?" She sobered. "I'm not going to kiss you here. I'm not going to hold your hand. Did it ever occur to you that it's my first day on the job, and I'm nervous? That I might like to have your help? Have a friend at my side? That no one would think that was weird?"

Her voice sounded a bit pinched, and Andrew's heart filled with affection for her. "I'm sorry," he murmured. "Honest, I am."

She nodded, stood, and smoothed down her dress. "Okay."

He stood too, the words he wanted to say piling up in his throat. He opened his mouth and said, "Did it ever occur to you that I'm dying to kiss you, and every time we're together, my thoughts wander that way?"

Her eyes dropped to his mouth, and Andrew thought she wanted to kiss him too. "How about dinner at my place tonight?"

"Do you cook?"

"It has been a very long time since I've dated anyone," she said, a bit of nervous energy infecting the air between them. "I don't know why I said that. Only that I think you should know."

"Is that your way of telling me I can't kiss you tonight?"

She swallowed and wiped her hands down her dress again. "I don't know," she said.

"I haven't dated anyone in a while either," he said. "And dinner tonight sounds great. You didn't answer if you could cook."

"I'm okay in the kitchen," she said. "We can order in, if you'd like."

"I can pick something up, if you want."

"I like that Chinese take-out over by the gas station."

"Harry Wong's. I'll swing by there and come over about seven?"

She nodded, and Andrew walked around his desk to stand right in front of her. He took both of her hands in his, a thrill running from the top of his skull to the soles of his feet. It zinged around after that, causing him to smile.

"Carla will see," Becca murmured, swaying slightly.

Andrew went with her, keeping both eyes past her on his secretary. She had the phone to her ear, completely unconcerned about what was transpiring in the office behind her. "I'll close my blinds next time," he said.

He leaned down and pressed his lips to Becca's temple. A quick kiss, nowhere near the mark he wanted to hit, and released her.

"Let's go see this SonarBot," he said.

THE BASEMENT WAS UNUSUALLY QUIET TODAY, BUT GRAHAM SAT AT a chest-high counter, a tablet lying in front of him.

"Hey," Andrew said when he arrived at the counter. The tablet held a bunch of code he didn't understand.

Graham smiled as he looked up. "Hey, there." He stood. "I'm Graham Whittaker. You must be Becca Collings." He met Andrew's eye for much too long before focusing on Becca long enough to shake her hand.

"We're ready to see the bot," Andrew said, glad he'd disclosed to Becca that Graham knew about them. "And Becca will need anything you think is relevant to her preparing media statements, speeches, or press releases."

"I'll have Janet put it together," Graham said. "Let's go."

They left the main room of the basement and entered a much different area. Becca's step slowed as she drank in every detail.

"This is like being underground," she said, her voice awed.

"It's supposed to simulate that," Graham said. "So I designed this bot to use sonar to detect gas beneath layers of rock. It's tricky, because some of the types of rocks we have here in Wyoming, along with a lot of our other dig sites, block the sonar."

"They block it?" she asked.

"They absorb it," he corrected himself. "So we get back reads as if there's no gas there. But there is. Normally, we simply fracture down to find it. But with the SonarBot, we're trying to locate the gas before we mine for it." He pressed his palm to a reader and waited until it beeped.

The door opened, and he entered it. "So I started working with the rocks here in Wyoming. We went all over and got all the samples from our mining sites, and we built this simulation, I guess."

The layers and layers of rock had been reconstructed just as they were at the dig sites.

"I had to work layer by layer, figuring out how much sonar a particular type of rock could absorb, and what the readings would look like when they hit gas. It took a long time."

"A really long time," Andrew said.

Graham chuckled. "My brother doesn't understand the nuances of computer science. One change can mean thousands of lines of code need to be redone, or written anew, or whatever."

"It's the whatever I don't get," Andrew said.

"Anyway," Graham said as he moved over to the plastic case where they kept SonarBot. "I finally came up with the right sequencing. The right level of sonar to get through the layers of rock here in Wyoming. And we developed the SonarBot." He stood in front of it, a remarkable little robot that somehow Andrew wished was bigger.

For the amount they'd spent to design and build it—both in terms of money and time—it should be the size of the Sears Tower.

As it was, the SonarBot was about four feet long and three feet wide. Barely a kid's toy. It had big, bulky wheels perfect for the terrain it would be traversing, and then it was basically a computer box, with screens on the top to show readings.

"Do you have to go with it?" Becca asked, peering down into the case. Her face held wonder and excitement, and Andrew started to feel those same things in his pulse. This was an amazing thing. It would improve their business, make it more profitable, and help the people of Wyoming.

"Nope," Graham said. "We can set up a mobile lab anywhere. Even just in a room at a school, or an office at the town hall. We can make him move with a remote, and send out the sonar with a press of a button."

"Show her the simulation," Andrew said, a hint of pride welling in him and he hadn't even designed the darn thing.

Graham turned to the huge screens behind SonarBot, which they'd used to present the robot to their family and the top scientists at the company. No one else knew about it yet, and they'd get all the details only an hour before the official unveiling.

"We went out with it oh, what? Two dozen times?"

"Probably," Andrew said. He wasn't the scientist. He didn't take the notes. At the end there, he'd stopped driving out into the Wyoming wilderness just to have the robot fail again. But not Graham. The man was as dedicated as anyone could possibly be to getting SonarBot to work.

"We recorded every time, made notes, analyzed what was happening. Tested here. Adjusted. Reworked things. And went out again." He flipped open the wall panel and pressed a button.

The screen brightened, and he said, "Play SonarBot, final excursion."

The video began, and it showed the robot rumbling along the Wyoming rocks at quite a steady clip.

"Whoa," Becca said. "How fast does it go?"

"Up to forty miles per hour," Graham said.

The robot slowed and Graham said, "We use a frequency of 200 hertz, and we've tried to use the sound waves at a low decibel so we don't disrupt nearby communities."

"What's it at?"

A loud *ping!* went out from the SonarBot on the screen, and Becca jumped.

"We've committed to it being no louder than one-hundred-ten decibels," Graham said. "The average rock concert is up to one-hundred-fourteen."

"Not a lot of rock concerts in Wyoming," Becca mumbled as she stepped closer to the screen. "Are these the readings?"

The video had changed to a top-only view of SonarBot, with the five screens for findings.

"Yes," Graham said. "We get depth, type of substance." He pointed to the second row. "So we see here that it hits gas and the returning echoes are at a different wavelength." He moved down a notch. "This is the depth. And this is the volume. Once the SonarBot finds gas, it goes back and forth until the entire pocket is mapped."

He tapped the wall and the video sped up. He tapped again and a moment later, a diagram came up. "See? There's the pocket we mapped on our last trial. Now we know exactly where to dig. We do the hydraulic fracturing in the biggest concentration and we can get all the gas out with one mine instead of multiple."

The screen darkened, and he said, "Lights, level one," and the room brightened again.

Becca looked at him, then Andrew, then SonarBot.

"So," Andrew said, his pulse humming along at quite the clip. "What do you think?" He exchanged a glance with Graham. Becca's opinion was very important, as she had been one of the most vocal against what Springside had been doing.

She looked back at Andrew. "What do I think? I think this is the most brilliant thing I've ever seen."

A smile burst onto his face. "Yeah?"

"I think your protests will stop now, Mister Whittaker."

Andrew tipped his head back and laughed. "Good, because it's part of your job to make sure everything is presented to the public in the best light possible. Can you give me a second with Graham? You can wait just outside and we'll go back up to the office together." He gestured for her to leave the room first, which she did.

"So?" he asked Graham. "Hiring her was a good move, right?"

Graham shook his head as he chuckled. "Andrew, you tell yourself what you need to tell yourself."

"What does that mean?"

"It means you're head over heels for her, and you've been out once."

"I am not. Let's focus on the SonarBot. She liked it, and she's been protesting against our company for a decade, Graham. A *decade.*"

"That's because she didn't like Dad."

Andrew's blood froze in his veins. "What?"

"She didn't like Dad. They got into a fight or something years ago."

"How do you know that?" Andrew hadn't lived in Coral Canyon for a while, and he admittedly didn't know much about Springside before Graham had called and begged him to come be the public relations director for the company.

Graham shrugged like this information was no big deal. But it was to Andrew. "I don't know. Dad told me? Maybe Dwight did. Maybe I read about it. But it's good she likes the concept."

Andrew followed his brother out of the lab and went with Becca back up to his office, his mind whirring. He'd ask her that night, over Chinese food. After all, he did really like her and he didn't want any secrets between them.

CHAPTER 10

Becca's first day ended much better than it had started. That SonarBot was cool, and while she spent the remainder of the afternoon with yet more paper to look at, the unveiling of the robot was actually going to be fun.

She made a couple of checklists, took the thumb drive home with her though she wasn't sure when she'd have time to look at it, and had just managed to feed all the strays and changed her clothes before Andrew arrived with the food.

Otto barked, but she pushed him out of the doorway so Andrew could come in. "I'm not the cleanest person in town," she said. "Otto, back *up*." She gave the huge Lab another push and he finally fell back a few steps.

Andrew grinned at her, and he hadn't even changed his clothes from earlier that day. "In the kitchen with this?"

"Yes, through there." She pointed though it was unnecessary. The living room connected to the kitchen with a cut-out in the wall to allow conversation to flow through. She had two barstools at the bar, though she never ate there.

Otto, ever the animal to go wherever food could be found, trotted after Andrew. Becca adjusted her shirt, pulling it down over the waistband of her jeans. She was *tired,* and maybe inviting Andrew over for dinner had been a mistake.

A yawn overtook her right as he came back into the living room. "Tired?" he asked.

"Yes," she admitted. "I haven't worked that hard in a while." She settled onto one end of the couch though she was hungry and could probably eat enough to feed an army.

"Oh?" He joined her on the couch, the picture of perfection, right there in her living room.

"You haven't been home yet?"

"I have."

"You didn't change." She raised her eyebrows. "Do you wear a suit to bed, Mister Whittaker?"

"Very funny."

Becca thought so, and when he didn't answer her question, she started to wonder if he really didn't own a pair of pajamas. "Seriously, though. You have pajamas, right?" She loved the flirtatious energy between them, and Andrew wore a look of desire in his eyes when he looked at her again.

"Yes, Miss Nosy. I own pajamas."

"Do you wear them?"

"Yes."

"Why didn't you change then?"

"You ask so many questions."

"You like my questions."

"Not when they're about me." He stood and walked toward the kitchen. "I'm starving. Can we eat?"

She followed him, not quite ready to let this go. She got down a couple of plates from the cupboard. "You…intimidate me in the suit. I thought this was going to be personal time."

He caught her wrist as she reached into the silverware drawer for forks. The increase in electricity should've shorted out the light bulbs, but they continued to blaze evenly.

"I intimidate you?"

She locked her eyes onto his. "Just here, in my house. Not at work." My, he was gorgeous, and so close to her, and her mouth started watering for all the wrong reasons. "And, um." She swallowed back all that saliva. "I'm usually the one who intimidates men."

"You are?" He spoke so softly, almost tenderly.

"That's what I've been told." She shrugged, his fingers still tracing a circular pattern around her wrist. "I don't know. Something about how I know so many dumb facts, or that I won't let certain subjects drop."

He didn't need to know everything about her disastrous break up with Jarom right now. But her ex *had* told her that he didn't like that she was smarter than him, and she'd challenged him with, "What am I supposed to do? Act dumb?"

"I think smart is sexy," Andrew said, stepping closer and moving both hands to her waist. He drew her effortlessly into his embrace, and Becca sighed as she pressed her cheek to his chest.

It seemed strange that less than a week ago, she was jobless, prospectless—both on the job front and the boyfriend front—and just…less than she felt now. Happiness coiled through her, and she wanted to stay in Andrew's arms for a good long while.

He, however, seemed to have a serious need to eat, because he stepped back only a few seconds later and started dishing himself some of the tiny spicy chicken that was her favorite too.

"Tell me something about you I don't know," she said.

He cast her a wary look and went for the ham fried rice. "I didn't change my clothes before I came, because my only other options are what I wear to feed the horses."

Her eyebrows went up. "How many horses?"

"Thirteen of them," he said. "Every morning. I've given up on the nighttime feeding. I have a man named Jake for that."

She spooned a healthy portion of noodles onto her plate to go with her chicken. "And you like taking care of the horses?"

"Very much."

"Do you ride?"

"Yes."

"How often?"

He gave her a look that said *Is this Twenty Questions?* but then answered her with, "Every weekend."

"Huh."

"Huh, what?"

She finished filling her plate and took it around the wall to the bar. He joined her, and she said, "I'd love to go horseback riding on the weekends."

"Oh, you would, would you?"

"Is that something you'd consider? Me coming with you?" She speared a piece of chicken but didn't put it in her mouth. "And you know, I'm doing all the asking for dates. I think I'm going to stop doing that."

Andrew had bypassed the forks and unwrapped a pair of chopsticks instead. He held them loosely in his fingers, his attention solely on her.

"Becca," he said.

She waited, expecting more than just her name. "Yeah?" she asked when he still said nothing.

"Are you sure I can't kiss you tonight?"

"I never said you couldn't." But fear bolted through her with the power of a freight train. "I just—I mean—I might not be very good at it."

He shook his head as he smiled. "Becca, you're good at everything you do."

"I—"

"And I would love for you to come riding with me this weekend." He mixed his chicken with his rice and popped a bite into his mouth.

She sighed, every muscle in her body releasing. "You're not a very nice man," she said.

"What?" He chuckled, because he knew exactly what.

"I thought you were going to kiss me," she said.

"Oh, really? I told you I was starving."

"Then you'll have bad breath. You think I want to be kissed after you eat this?" She put her spicy bite of chicken in her mouth. A moan followed, because the sauce was sweet and sticky, with the right amount of burn in the back of her throat.

She swallowed and said, "I don't think so."

Andrew laughed again, and Becca enjoyed the sound of it. Maybe not as much as she'd have enjoyed being kissed by him, but apparently they were going to eat first.

"How's your mom?" she asked, a question which drew Andrew's attention.

"She's...okay."

"I mean, I was thinking about her today when you and Beau were talking. I think it would be hard to lose a spouse, especially if it was sudden."

"It was difficult," he said. "On all of us."

She nodded, the moment between them turning tender and meaningful. "My family's from this tiny speck of a town out in the Devil's Tower area," she said. "Crystal Lake? Ever heard of it?"

"Have I ever heard of Crystal Lake? It's only the best place to go swimming in the summer."

Her whole body lit up. "You've been there?"

"My dad used to take us all at the end of June. We'd leave my mom home—something about her needing time to herself—and we'd camp, hike, fish, and swim." He wore pure joy on his face, and the love for his family shone through in the tone of his voice. "I love Crystal Lake."

"My father builds boats up there," she said. "With his bare hands."

Andrew looked at her. "Siblings?"

"Two younger brothers and a sister."

"So you're the oldest?"

"That's right." She twirled her fork in her noodles, suddenly glad Andrew was there to keep her company.

"No wonder you're so bossy." He nudged her with his knee,

and she jerked her head toward him only to find that sparkling tease in his eyes.

"You should hear yourself, Mister." She lowered her voice and spoke through pursed lips. "I need you to look over this agreement and make it comply with the law." She burst into laughter, thrilled when Andrew joined her.

She silenced when he trailed his fingertips down the side of her face and twirled a lock of her hair around his thumb.

"Have I said how beautiful I think you are?"

Becca's stomach tightened, and she shook her head.

"Well, I'm saying it now." He dropped his hand and looked back at his plate. "Can Otto eat people food?"

"You give him that and he'll be sick all night. Too spicy."

The yellow Lab sat at attention only a few feet away. Becca slid off the barstool and padded into the kitchen, glad to be rid of her heels. "Here. Feed him this." She got out a tub of sliced turkey, and Otto whined.

"Can he do any tricks?"

"Sit, stay, lay down, and high five," she said, wondering if Andrew was going to tease her all night for a kiss. He made Otto do several tricks, treating him with the turkey after each one.

She rinsed her plate, and then his, and joined him as he looked out the back window into her yard. "It's getting late," she said. "And now that I have a job, I actually have to go to bed on time."

"What's with all the cat bowls?" he asked.

"Oh, um." She squirmed beside him, and he slipped his arm around her waist. Everything calmed when before his touch had caused such excitement in her. She wondered what had changed, but she didn't have time to dwell on it.

"I feed strays," she said. "Dogs, cats, probably a family of raccoons."

"Raccoons are vicious animals," he murmured, the tip of his nose sliding down her cheek.

"I know," she whispered. "But if they're starving, they deserve to eat."

The rumble from his low chuckle moved from his chest into hers as he brought her closer to him again. "You have a soft heart," he said, not really asking.

"I don't like to see living things suffer," she admitted.

"I'm dying," he whispered.

"Then kiss me," she murmured back, her eyes already closed.

He took forever, but when his lips finally brushed against hers, the room filled with warmth and starlight though he pulled away quickly. She reached up to hold his face in her hands, wanting to set the pace and keep him as close as she wanted him until she was ready to let him go.

He touched his mouth to hers again, and this time he didn't let go. She kissed him back, her need and want for him stronger than she'd admitted to herself. She slowed the movement and broke the connection.

"Becca?" he asked, his breathing quick and his forehead pressed to hers. "You did great."

She scoffed and swatted at his chest, but he held her tight in his arms, his laughter low and ending quickly. Their eyes met, and Becca couldn't comprehend that this was her reality. He was the absolute last person she would've imagined herself with. But the chemistry between them had been strong since the first time they'd met, like something had just clicked into place.

"How was my breath?" he asked, still teasing her.

"I didn't notice. We better try again." She tipped up on her toes and kissed him, his lips the most delicious she'd ever tasted.

CHAPTER 11

Andrew had not kissed a woman in quite a long time. His heartbeat raced, and the feel of her in his arms brought him so much comfort. It seemed strange that he'd met her less than a week ago, and here he stood in her house, kissing her.

And kissing her, and kissing her.

He finally came to his senses and pulled away, wanting to be a gentleman but also needing her to know how much he liked her without having to put it into words.

Becca tucked herself against his chest and they faced the window together as the last of the sunlight disappeared. He liked that she fed strays, that she had a kind heart for those in need, whether human or feline or canine. Or whatever raccoons were.

"Okay, so I better go," he finally said with a sigh. "Your second day isn't going to be any easier than the first."

She walked him to the door, slid her hands over his shoulders, and smiled at him in a slightly woozy way. She was tired, but Andrew couldn't help kissing her one last time before ducking out into the night.

He felt the exhaustion pulling through him too, and the thought of getting up early in the morning to feed the horses made him cranky as he drove back to the lodge. So did the dark windows. Even the strip at the bottom of Bree's door was black, and Andrew entered his own room, finding that he wanted to talk with someone about his relationship with Becca.

When he'd dated in high school, he used to sit up with his mother, and he could practically hear what she'd tell him.

Is she nice, Andrew?

Are you being nice to her?

What are you worried about?

Andrew brushed his teeth, admitting to himself that he was worried about how he could manage everything at work—including Becca—without anyone finding out that he'd kissed her. There were already a million little pieces and details to be managed, and he was bound to forget something.

But he couldn't forget to sleep, so he crawled into bed and fell into unconsciousness with the taste of Becca still in his mouth.

The next day, she once again arrived at the office before he did. He caught sight of her sitting at her desk as he went next door. "Morning," he called, flinging his hand out in a haphazard wave.

He didn't stop walking, so he hit his hand on the doorframe as he entered his office. "Ow!" Frustration and humiliation raced through him simultaneously, and he ignored Carla's call asking if he was okay.

The hours at work passed quicker than ever, as if God wanted to test Andrew to see if he could meet the October first deadline for the reveal. Becca was a huge help, because she learned quickly, worked as hard as he did, and asked questions he hadn't considered.

He spent every evening with her as they sampled the cuisine from a different restaurant each night. On Saturday, he fed the horses and promised Wolfgang he'd be back to ride tomorrow, then he zipped down into town to have lunch with his mother.

He hadn't brought up Admiral Church, and he wasn't the

only one at lunch. The whole family—minus Eli in California—was there, as if it were their Saturday night dinner tradition. He wanted to ask his mom about this Admiral guy despite Beau's assurances that he was a good man.

When he walked into the house, it was clear he was the last to arrive and that lunch was about to be served. His mom stood in front of a Crock pot with a fork and a bottle of barbecue sauce.

"Hey, Ma," he said, stepping up to her and placing a kiss on her cheek. "Pulled pork sandwiches?" His stomach growled.

"There you are. I just asked Beau to text you to see if you were coming." She glanced up at him, and it was like looking into his own eyes. "He thought you might be working today."

"Not today," he said, though he had loads of items still on his to-do list at work. "Maybe next weekend though."

"Laney, we're ready."

She stood from the table and left her phone, which she'd been looking at. She stepped over to the back door and opened it, calling, "Graham! Bailey! Time for lunch."

"What can I do to help?" Andrew asked.

"Go sit." She lifted the pot out of the heater and took it to the table. Andrew followed with the buns and as they passed, she added, "And don't ask me about my date tonight." She looked at him sternly, and Andrew tossed the buns on the table beside the meat.

"Why not?"

"I don't want to talk about it."

"Well, I think that says something."

She walked over to the edge of the kitchen and said, "Beau, lunch," and turned back. "We haven't even gone out yet."

"But you said yes, Mom. So you must see something you like." Even the thought of his mother kissing Admiral the way he had Becca.... Andrew shook his head, needing that image out of his head.

"He's a nice guy," she said.

"Who is?" Beau asked.

"No one," she said at the same time Andrew said, "Admiral Church."

"I told you not to ask her about it."

"I didn't. She brought him up." Andrew gave his brother a glare as Graham entered the house with a burst of laughter, his step-daughter right behind him.

"Graham, will you say grace?" Andrew's mother moved away from Andrew and Beau and took a seat at the table.

"What did I interrupt?" he asked, switching his gaze from person to person.

"Nothing," Andrew said as he turned away from Beau's unhappy expression.

"Laney?"

"Your mother's date tonight."

Graham pulled a chair out directly across from their mother. "You have a date tonight?" His tone was one of incredulous surprise.

"Thank you," Andrew said triumphantly. He reached for the bowl of macaroni salad. "I think it says something that you didn't tell any of us, Mom."

"It doesn't say anything." She swatted his hand. "Graham's going to say grace."

Graham waited for Beau to join them, then he thanked the Lord for their food, their family, the weather, and Coral Canyon.

"Why didn't you tell us?" Graham asked as if the conversation about their mother's date hadn't stopped.

"Because." She sighed and took the twist tie off the bag of buns. "It's my first date since your dad died, and I thought you might react this way." She gave Andrew specifically a glare. "And I'm not sure how I feel about it, or if it will even turn into anything. I guess I didn't see the point."

Graham didn't say anything as he loaded his bun with twice the amount of meat it needed. Beau likewise continued filling his plate with food. Andrew didn't have to understand her reasons to accept them, so he said, "Fair enough."

"Why don't you tell them about your press secretary?" Graham asked, and Andrew choked on his forkful of macaroni salad. Horror sang through him as he stared at his oldest brother. Heat rose through him, and there was no way his face wasn't bright red.

"Nothing to tell," he said after clearing his airway of the offending noodles.

Beau started laughing, which grated against Andrew's nerves. "Oh, I believe him. Don't you, Mom?"

"I'm sure if Andrew has something to tell us, he will."

Andrew had never loved his mother more, and he regretted his ire with her for keeping her date a secret. He simply hadn't known she even wanted to date again, and most days, he did just fine without missing his father too much.

But sometimes, the fact that his dad wasn't there hit him hard, and he spent quite a while thinking about fishing with his dad, and the times on the lake, or lessons he taught as they worked cutting tree limbs or ridding the lawn of weeds.

He'd eaten half his sandwich before Beau said, "Lindsey saw you getting quite a huge order from the deli a couple of nights ago."

"So?" Andrew asked. "Is it a crime to eat two sandwiches for dinner? I work over ten hours a day."

Beau did too, but he simply smiled as if he knew the vegetarian delight had been for Becca, and that Andrew had stayed at her place until almost midnight before he'd trudged on back to the lodge.

But it somehow felt bigger and more empty than ever, and he didn't like being there alone.

"Eli's coming for Christmas," his mother said, and that got Andrew's attention.

"Are we doing the tree lighting?" he asked. Graham had started the tradition two years ago, and it somehow meant a lot to Andrew.

"You live at the lodge," Graham said. "It's up to you."

"I'll make sure I figure it out," he said. "I'll be gone for three weeks in October."

"You'll still have two months before Christmas," Beau said. "How hard is it to flip a switch?"

"Beau," his mother chastised. "It's more than that, and you know it. He has to get the tree, decorate it, arrange dinner with Celia, the gift exchange."

Andrew's head hurt just thinking about making more plans, for another big event. But this was his family, and he wanted them all at the lodge with him. "I'll make it happen," he said. "And I'll make sure to tell Bree not to overbook us."

"I'll come up for Christmas Eve," his mom said. "Beau?"

"We'll see," he said. "I've got a new case I should have started by then."

"You won't work it on Christmas Eve, will you?" Andrew asked.

"It's a unique case," Beau said evasively, and Andrew let it drop. He'd save a room for Beau too, who'd stayed last year.

He stayed quiet for the rest of lunch, his mind whirring about going out into the forest to chop down a Christmas tree with Becca. And then decorating the tree with hot chocolate sitting on the mantle—and Becca at his side. And their fabulous Christmas Eve dinner for friends and family after the tree lighting—and of course, Becca would be at that too.

He wasn't going to see her that day, as they'd spent so many hours together both at work and in the evenings this week. But as lunch ended and everyone dispersed, he sat in his sensible sedan and sent her a message.

Want to go horseback riding today?

CHAPTER 12

By the time Becca checked her phone, Andrew's invitation to go horseback riding was a half an hour old. She wiped her hair off her sweaty forehead, thinking about how long it would take her to shower and drive out to the lodge.

But she wouldn't need to shower if she went horseback riding. Would she?

Sure, she typed out. *Sorry, I was in the backyard getting everything ready for winter.* It would hopefully be the last time she'd have to mow and weed and clip back her bushes and vines.

He didn't answer immediately, and she thought she'd missed her opportunity to see him that day. They hadn't said anything about living their own lives this weekend, but it had somehow just been an unspoken agreement.

He'd mentioned something about lunch with his mother, and she did what she normally did on weekends when she had a job: housework or yard work.

She hadn't ridden a horse for a while, probably since leaving Crystal Lake. And she really couldn't picture Andrew in anything but a suit and tie, those shiny shoes peeking out from beneath his cuffs.

Her phone buzzed and she almost pulled a muscle in her

neck in her haste to look. Andrew had said, *Do you know where Whiskey Mountain Lodge is?*

Yes.

I live there. Stables in the back. Text me when you get here and I'll come meet you.

She opened her maps app and put in the lodge and learned that it sat twenty-five minutes from her house.

The clock read two-forty-five, but she felt the need to bring something to eat. He'd shown up at her house with food every night for the past five days in a row. And she wanted to shower so she would look and smell nice for Andrew, but she didn't want to bathe now and again later.

So she grabbed some gum and changed out her sneakers for an old pair of cowgirl boots before getting in her car and starting the drive out to the lodge.

Whiskey Mountain Lodge had burned several years ago, but the building she pulled up to showed no signs of that. It was beautiful and majestic, the Teton Mountains standing right behind it as if to protect it from any further damage.

"This is where he lives?" She knew the energy company was profitable, and would certainly continue to be once the SonarBot came out. But she had no idea he could afford a place like this— and the shoes and suits he wore.

She suddenly didn't feel so bad about the salary she'd requested and a bit worse about having him over to her inferior house for the past week.

I'm here, she texted, and the front door of the lodge opened at the same time she closed her car door behind her. A man stood there wearing jeans and a cowboy hat, and it took her several long seconds to realize it was Andrew.

A smile exploded across her face, and she didn't think it was possible to find him more attractive than she did in the fancy suits and ties, his hair swept devilishly to the side.

But this cowboy version of the public relations director had her pulse in a tizzy. Thankfully, her legs still operated just fine and they got her up the steps and into his arms. "Don't you look country?" She laughed and he joined in with her.

"I told you I take care of the horses here."

"I suppose I just couldn't imagine it." She stood back and took in the red plaid shirt, which somehow completed the look. "So I guess you really are a cowboy."

"When I have to be." He laced his fingers through hers and led her back down the steps instead of going into the lodge. A twinge of disappointment cut through her that she wouldn't get to see the inside of the lodge, but she told herself to be patient.

"Celia's in there," he said by way of explanation. "And if we want to keep this—" He lifted their joined hands. "A secret, she probably shouldn't know about it."

"Celia Armstrong?"

"Yeah, she's the lodge cook."

"You mean your personal cook," she wasn't asking, and plenty of playfulness entered her tone.

"Not really," he said. "She cooks for family meals and things like that. Graham hired her to cook for the guests at the lodge." He cut her a look out of the side of his eye. "We have guests that stay on the top floor and in the basement."

"So you have the whole main floor?"

"Well, me and Bree."

Becca stopped walking though the stables were in sight down the hill a bit. "You and Bree?" She didn't shrill out the words, but she didn't know he had a female roommate. "You failed to mention her."

"She's our groundskeeper and decorator," he said, giving her a quizzical look. "I told you about her."

"Not that she lived here. Celia doesn't live here, does she?"

"Well, no. She stays over sometimes though, if the weather's bad."

Becca cut him a glance out of the corner of her eye. "Then why does Bree live here?"

"She does all the landscaping and gardening. Oh, and she

took over Eli's job of booking the lodge and is our event director too." He shrugged, seemingly undisturbed that he lived with this woman. "So it makes sense for her to live on-site."

"Who is this 'our'?"

He started walking again, slower than before. "Graham bought the lodge when he moved back to Coral Canyon, but he married Laney and lives down the road at her ranch. He brought all of us home—well, me and Eli—to help with the lodge and the energy company so he could focus on his robotics. Making the lodge a vacation destination was really Eli's pet project, and he left a few months ago for California."

"You miss him?"

"Sure, I guess."

There was something more there that he wasn't saying, but Becca didn't know what question to ask to draw it out of him.

"So...Bree, how close is her room to yours?" Why Becca cared, she wasn't sure.

"Just down the hall." He paused outside the stable doors and looked at her, his eyes keen and searching.

"What?" she asked.

"You're jealous."

"Uh, yeah. I just found out my handsome cowboy boyfriend lives with another woman."

He reached up and cradled her face in his palm. "It's not like that, Becca. You know that, right?"

"Mm hm," she said, because he was moments from kissing her, and she didn't believe that he could kiss her with as much care and passion as he did and like another woman.

"Because it's not like that," he said. "Not even close. She works for our family."

Becca leaned away from him, causing him to drop his hand. "*I* work for you," she said, searching his face for more of an explanation.

He blinked as he realized his mistake. "Well, that's different." He reached for the door to the stable.

"How so?" she asked, following him inside.

"You don't live here."

Becca didn't quite get what the difference was. But he stopped in front of a tall horse and said, "You'll ride this one. Her name is Second to Caroline. She's Eli's favorite horse."

"Which is your favorite?"

He immediately walked down the aisle and lifted his hand to stroke a brown and white horse. She followed him and read the nameplate on the outside of the stall. "Wolfgang."

"Wolfy for short." He gazed up at the horse with adoration in his eyes, and Becca memorized that softness there, hoping he'd look at her like that later today, preferably right before he kissed her.

He led the horses outside and saddled them, impressing her with his cowboy skills. "All right," he said. "Up you go."

Becca searched her memory for how to get on a horse. She hesitated too long, because Andrew said, "Left foot here," and tapped the stirrup on the side of the horse closest to her. "Push yourself up. Throw your leg over."

Becca put her foot where he said, but it felt like her knee was all the way to her chin. She bounced on her foot and pushed, but she didn't get anywhere.

Andrew burst out laughing, and Becca stumbled with her left foot still in that blasted stirrup.

"Whoa," he said as if she were the horse, and dashed behind her so he could catch her should she fall. The strength of his body behind her brought her comfort and relief, but she didn't lose the battle to gravity.

She did get her foot out of the stirrup, and said, "I think I need a box." Her brothers had helped her younger sister onto a horse with an apple box.

"Oh, no you don't. I'll help you." He edged in closer behind her, leaving very little room between her and him, as well as her and the horse. "Foot up," he said, his voice rumbling through her back.

Please don't let me mess up again, she prayed as she put her foot in the stirrup. He counted down, and she jumped, feeling his hands tighten on her waist as he practically threw her up. She managed to get her other leg over and onto the horse, a feeling of triumph spreading through her.

He swung onto his horse with little effort, and they set off for the tree line. "How long since you've ridden?"

"Is it that obvious?"

"You're gripping those reins like they'll save you." He grinned at her, and she tried to relax.

"It's been a while," she admitted, chancing a glance at him.

"Well, it's a lot like kissing then. You're doing great."

"Ha ha," she said, only not rolling her eyes because she was worried she might lose her balance if she didn't stare straight ahead. "Very funny."

He continued to chuckle, and Becca liked the sound of his throaty laughter and the sight of him atop that pretty horse. As they walked beneath the limbs and among the pines, Becca couldn't recall a time when she felt happier.

If she could hold onto this feeling—and him—for another couple of weeks, her relationship with Andrew would be one of her longest. As they settled into silence, her worries became full-fledged. What if they broke up before the tour? How awkward would that be? Would she even have a job?

She tried to push her rotating thoughts away and enjoy the horseback ride with her secret cowboy billionaire boyfriend, but they would only go so far.

———

"Do you need this scarf?" Raven held up a navy and white polka-dotted thing that Becca had charged to Springside Energy and never worn.

"I don't know." Becca felt completely out of control with two suitcases open on her bed and the tour starting the following day right there in Coral Canyon with a huge press conference on the steps of City Hall.

She turned in a circle, trying to remember what she had been looking for when Raven asked about the scarf.

Her dark-haired friend stepped in front of her and put her hands on Becca's shoulders. Raven's nearly black eyes searched Becca's lighter ones. "I've never seen you like this. Even when we were planning that big march in Cheyenne."

Becca didn't want to think about that. That had been a worthless protest that had taken her somewhere she hadn't wanted to go. But she had been nervous, because she knew she shouldn't have been going to Cheyenne.

Did that mean she wasn't supposed to go on this tour with Andrew? Their relationship had survived the last two weeks. More than survived. Thrived. She liked him, really liked him, and the feeling seemed to be mutual.

"Talk to me," Raven said.

"I'm nervous because I'm dating Andrew Whittaker," she blurted.

Raven's eyes widened and she fell back several steps until she hit the window seat. She sank to a sitting position and asked, "You want to run that by me again?"

"Andrew and I are dating."

"Your boss?" Raven wore a strange sort of smile. Almost giddy, and yet still a bit horrified. "You're dating your boss."

"He's not my boss. We work together." Becca turned away from her best friend, feeling a bit calmer now that someone knew.

"How long has this been going on?"

"Our first date was the day we went shopping."

Becca jumped to her feet. "You've been dating him for weeks! Why didn't you tell me?" She seemed hurt and yet excited at the same time. "I feel like an idiot now, trying to get you to double with me and Matt."

"No, no, it's fine." Becca picked up two socks that matched

and balled them before throwing them in one of her suitcases. She'd mostly be wearing heels but she'd brought her running shoes and planned to use the hotel gyms if she needed to work off some extra anxiety.

"Have you kissed him?"

Becca shrugged, all the answer Raven needed to shriek.

"Becca, this is huge." She moved to stand beside her again. "I can see why you're nervous."

"Why is this huge?"

"Oh, let's see. You haven't dated anyone since Jarom, and that guy was totally not worth the time you mourned him. Second, he's the only man you've dated longer than a month, and you're almost there with Andrew now."

Becca knew. Though she didn't want to, she'd been counting the days, almost expecting Andrew to break things off by day twenty. Or twenty-one. But it was twenty-three now, and they were going on a three-week tour together tomorrow. Would that take them to forty-four days, and if so, how much longer would it last? Christmas? Could she make it to Christmas before she drove him away?

"I can see this isn't all about the tour." Raven abandoned the folding and sorting and packing of clothes.

"Of course it's not." Becca picked up a blouse and put it down again, not in the right frame of mind to decide if she needed it or not. She couldn't sit on the bed because of all the clothes and bags. "I'm not sure I can keep his attention for much longer."

"Becca," Raven said reprovingly. "Of course you can. You're the smartest woman I know."

"He's smart too."

"So what?" Raven brushed Becca's hair off her shoulder. "That just means he knows what a gem you are."

"I'll annoy him eventually. Too many questions." She shook her head, remembering a few days ago when she'd taken her list into his office and bothered him until he'd answered all her questions. He'd once told her to ask anything she wanted, that he needed her to so he could see situations from all sides.

"Becca—"

Thankfully, Becca's phone rang, interrupting Raven's reassurance. "It's Andrew. Excuse me." She took a few steps away from her best friend and faced the window. "Hey." She wasn't sure if she sounded softer or happy to hear from him or not, but Raven giggled behind her.

"You got arrested in Cheyenne?" he practically barked.

"Yes, I mean, it wasn't really an arrest."

"Why didn't you tell me this before? I can't *believe* I'm hearing about this the night before our announcement."

"Why does it matter?" she asked, her defenses flying into place. "I spent the night in jail with over two hundred other people. They didn't book us or file charges. It was a stupid march. No one got hurt."

"It matters because the press secretary for Springside Energy will be under scrutiny from every county and every energy company starting at eight a.m. tomorrow." He huffed out his breath. "We need to meet and discuss damage control. Maybe write a quick piece about what it was and why it doesn't matter."

"I haven't packed—"

"I'll be there in ten minutes." He hung up, leaving Becca with a stone in her chest where her heart used to be.

She turned back to Raven, her phone hanging loosely in her hand at her side. "He found out about Cheyenne."

"I'm surprised he didn't know already."

"He didn't ask. I didn't have to do a background check." She felt like crying, but she lifted her chin. "He'll be here in a few minutes. You'll probably want to go."

Raven gripped her in a tight hug and said, "He likes you. It will work out."

Becca nodded and gave her friend a quick smile, wishing her

mom was there to point her wooden spoon at the Collings family motto: *Things always work out for us.*

She had it painted on barn slats, in vinyl letters on a rock in their front garden, and had made keychains for all the kids one year for Christmas when Becca was seventeen.

Raven left, and Becca followed her out into the living room so she could get things worked out with Andrew and their tour.

CHAPTER 13

A ndrew took the steps to Becca's front door in two leaps, pausing before he could bang down the door. But seriously? An arrest. How had he missed that?

You're angry at yourself, he told himself. *Calm down.*

He glanced up into the sky and prayed *Help me speak kindly.*

He couldn't think of much else to pray for, so he reached over and pressed the doorbell, something he'd done over a dozen times now, usually with a bag of food in his hand and anticipation building in his stomach for when he'd get to kiss Becca again.

He wasn't thinking about kissing now.

She opened the door, her chin already lifted and her eyes blazing. "Come in," she said in a professional voice. "I have everything on the computer for you."

Andrew tried to tame his glare, but from Becca's stoic expression, he hadn't succeeded. She turned and walked into her house, leaving him to follow her. No hello. No smile or squeal of delight at seeing him.

He really didn't like this tension between them, but he went into the living room and sat in front of the laptop she had open on the counter. "I'm going to go pack." She disappeared, and

Andrew peered at the screen, an image of a lot of people marching down the street, carrying protest signs not all unlike the one that had hit him a few weeks ago.

He recognized this march, and it had to do with equal rights —a worthy cause. So why had she been arrested?

The article didn't say much, only that a few hundred people had been taken in for questioning. They were held overnight and released, and his anger simmered away into frustration and then foolishness.

She hadn't really been arrested, just as she'd said. "Becca," he called, not wanting to go into her bedroom.

"Yeah?" She walked down the hall and paused at the edge of the living room.

"Why would Stuart Musgrove call me and say you'd been arrested?" He stood from the counter, curiosity burning through him now. "On a Sunday, no less."

"The day before the tour starts." Becca's voice sounded a bit hollow, and her eyes had glazed over at the first mention of Stuart's name. She snapped back to attention and looked at him. "Do you think he knows about the robot?"

"No." Andrew shook his head with complete confidence. "We've kept that knowledge under lock and key. Need-to-know basis only."

"Then it has to do with me," she said.

"Everyone would know about the press conference tomorrow, and you're listed as the first speaker."

She looked like she was about to be sick, what with her face all pale like that. "I went out with Stuart a couple of times," she said. "Maybe three. He was…insufferable. When he called to ask me out again, I said no."

Andrew's eyebrows went up and he took another step toward Becca. "Insufferable?"

"He's a know-it-all." Becca waved her hand dismissively. "It was just after the march, so he knew I'd spent the night in jail."

Andrew tilted his head, wondering what that night would've

been like. "Any other marches or fake arrests I need to know about?"

"Probably," Becca said. "Didn't you say our worst dirt would be thrown at us on this tour?"

That he had, but he also thought he'd known what the mudballs would be made of. This news of her being taken in for questioning after a rights march had set him all the way to hot in a single breath.

"I'm almost done packing," she said. "I'll be ready in the morning." She turned to go down the hall.

"Becca."

She paused, but she didn't look at him. Something had changed between them now that he'd called angry, now that he'd let his emotions show, now that he'd indicated that he didn't trust her.

You've always let your emotions show when it comes to Becca. In fact, he was able to be himself around her, one of the things he liked most about her. She never judged him when he griped about the accounting department. Consoled him when one of the biggest towns near their dig sites had refused to let them come speak at an official city event.

Becca had been the one to suggest holding an event under two huge white tents, with hot chocolate and pastries, to talk to the people on Musgrove Creek about the robot. Not only that, she'd coordinated the whole thing. Rented the tents. Ordered the food. Printed up flyers and made digital ad materials for their social media.

"Thanks for stopping by," she said, walking away. He stood in her living room for another few moments, but she didn't come back. Her message was clear—*show yourself out, Andrew.*

So he did, wishing he could apologize for the accusatory nature of his phone call and visit. He flipped his phone over in his hand. Over and over. Finally, he called Graham, who probably wouldn't answer as it was Sunday afternoon nap time at the ranch where he lived.

"Hey," he said in a whisper. "What's up?"

"Real quick: Is it lame to send an apology in a text?"

"To who?"

"Becca."

"Yes."

"Okay, thanks." Andrew hung up and looked at Becca's front door. He'd tell her tomorrow. He still had all of his own packing to do, another brief to read, and he needed to go over his speech with Celia.

So he backed out of Becca's driveway and headed back to the lodge, the weight of the tour feeling as big as the earth. And because he was nowhere near as strong as Atlas, one wrong step would send everything crashing down.

———

THE FOLLOWING MORNING, HE PARKED BEHIND THE CITY BUILDINGS, in a parking lot with a security guard. When he got out of his car, he was twenty minutes early for the agreed-upon time he and Becca would meet. Yet she clicked toward him in a navy blue dress with wide, sweeping white flowers on it. Her heels were practical and business-like. Her makeup professional. Her hair actually not quite as haphazard as he'd seen it previously.

She was stunning and spectacular though the sun hadn't even come up yet. "Good morning," she said, handing him a to-go cup of coffee from The Jumping Bean. She didn't look like their little spat yesterday had caused her an ounce of trouble, and for the first time in his life, Andrew wished he could wear makeup to hide the exhaustion on his face.

"Morning." He sipped the coffee and found it exactly as he liked—cream and sugar and caramel. "Are we ready for today?"

She met his eye, something sparking in her gaze. "I am, Mister Whittaker. Did you get the last-minute changes to your speech I sent over?"

At midnight, and yes, he'd still been awake. "Yes, thank

you," he said formally. He wanted to take her hand in his and dart down the alley between the two buildings. Kiss her until all the tension bled from his shoulders and the words of his speech aligned.

Later, he told himself. They had this meeting this morning, and one scheduled in Jackson Hole for that afternoon. They'd spend the night there before heading to their next destination, and while they'd have a lot of support here due to every employee at Springside being in the crowd, the other cities and towns would contain less fanfare.

"Nervous?" she asked.

"Yes," he admitted. "You?"

She nodded, her throat working as she swallowed. "I really think you should speak first."

"We've been over it, Becca." He didn't mean to sound tired or short with her, but he was afraid he'd been both.

"Yes, sir." She turned away from him, so perfectly poised and professionally put together that his heart squeezed. She'd changed so much from the jean-clad, tree-hugger T-shirted woman he'd been smitten with the moment he'd bled because of her.

She had such a strong spirit, and Andrew really admired that. He caught up to her and touched her forearm. "Becca?"

"Yes?" She paused and looked at him. Even with her heels, he still stood a few inches taller than her.

"Would you mind if we had a quick prayer together before we go in?" His stomach felt like he'd tied it in knots and then eaten a meal the size of Thanksgiving. He'd never seen Becca at church, and they hadn't spoken about religion in their relationship yet. But he always prayed before a big speaking event, and he wanted her to know it.

"Of course." She glanced around. "Right here? Or do you want to go back to the car? Find a room just inside?"

He looked around too, and another car entered the manned

parking lot. "Maybe your car," he said. They went back to it, and she started it, sat in the driver's seat, and waited for him.

"Okay," he said, suddenly so much more nervous about this than the speech. "Lord, we're grateful that we could be here on this fine October day. Please bless each of us that we'll speak clearly, that the crowds will be kind, and that we can get along." Where the last words had come from, Andrew wasn't sure. Maybe straight from his heart.

"Amen," he said quickly, before more of what he felt in his heart could be voiced. He reached over and gripped Becca's hand. "I'm sorry," he said. "I made some assumptions about you I shouldn't have." Last night, and long before he'd officially met her.

She looked at him, and his heart pounded in his chest and up into his mouth. Would she not forgive him?

"I suppose we all make erroneous assumptions sometimes." She swallowed, leaned forward just enough to let him know she wanted him to kiss her, and waited.

Andrew kissed her quickly, glad that she'd given him another chance so easily. "I'm trying to see things from all sides," he said. "It's really hard sometimes."

"Yeah." She gazed out the windshield. "Especially if you don't even know how many sides there are." Something hid beneath her words, but Andrew wasn't sure what it was. His watch beeped, a calendar reminder that he should be at City Hall right now.

He took a deep breath. "Show time."

CHAPTER 14

W atching Andrew in action was a glorious thing. He knew everyone, and they all knew him. He was polished and perfect, his notes for his speech tucked under one arm. Becca marveled that a month ago, she'd have been in the crowd here, disgusted at how easily he smiled and shook hands with the mayor.

Frustrated that he and his company seemed to get everything they wanted. Annoyed that the media and photographers flocked around him like he was the President of the United States when he was really a nobody from an energy company no one had ever heard of. In a state most people didn't know existed.

But she didn't feel any of those things today. She wore a completely different ensemble than she would've otherwise, and she shook hands with the same people he did, accepting his introductions as the new press secretary.

She'd spoken with many of the people who greeted her, and she stepped over to the microphone with a man named Terry, who'd said he'd show her how to raise and lower it before the event started.

Her speech was memorized, and she set her folder on the

podium. Their travel itinerary was inside too, and she knew that after the press conference and official unveiling of SonarBot this morning, they'd have lunch with the Whittaker family and the entire mayor's office before getting in a car bound for Jackson Hole.

Another appointment for a press conference waited there just before the evening news would hit televisions, all according to Andrew's plans.

Just get through the next hour, she told herself, *changing her internal pep talk into a prayer. Help me get through the next hour. And then the next.*

Praying with Andrew had been thrilling in a spiritual kind of way that Becca had never experienced before. None of her previous relationships had ever gotten that intimate before they were over, and she imagined herself sitting next to him at church, where the whole town could see.

Of course, that couldn't happen for a while, as they needed to keep their hand-holding and kissing in secret for a while longer.

She sidled over to Andrew, who was speaking to a councilman and his wife.

"It's time," she said quietly, and Andrew wrapped up the conversation. They moved over to their seats, which would be moved to make way for the screen that was hidden behind the chairs for now. It had been mounted to the concrete last night, and Graham himself would pull it up to show the video of the SonarBot she'd seen in the lab at Springside Energy.

"Where's Graham?" Andrew muttered, scanning the people on the steps and those still taking their places. "Have you seen him?" He kept his smile in place, but Becca could feel the tension radiating from him.

"He's right there." She pointed to the oldest Whittaker brother as Graham stepped past a security guard and into the space reserved for those who needed to be in front of the cameras and crowd.

Andrew stood and shook his brother's hand. "Cutting it close, aren't we?"

"Ronnie had a tough night." Graham didn't look like anything in his life was tough, but now that Becca had more knowledge of him and his life, she knew that wasn't true.

"You're up, Becca," Andrew said as he retook his seat. "We start and end on time."

He'd said that so many times, Becca fell asleep with those words running in her mind. Okay, maybe not all the time, as he usually kissed her so completely before he stumbled out into the dark that she laid awake thinking about that before falling asleep.

"I have forty-two seconds," she muttered back to him, which caused him to chuckle. At least maybe then he'd relax.

Becca felt like an army of fire ants had decided her stomach and digestive track would be a good place to take up residence. Her guts burned and writhed at the same time, and when her timer ticked to zero, she stood and approached the podium.

Her smile felt real as she beamed out at the crowd. She saw a lot of familiar faces, having lived in Coral Canyon for a while now. It helped that the entire staff of Springside Energy sat in the first few rows, and Carla's face was a particularly bright spot.

"Good morning, ladies and gentlemen. My name is Rebecca Collings, and I get the great pleasure of welcoming you to a special presentation by Springside Energy here at City Hall today."

She paused, took a breath, and told herself to speak slower. "Some of you might be a little surprised to see me on this side of the podium, when I'm usually out there." She nodded toward the back of the crowd. "And usually with a protest sign."

The audience twittered, a few laughs and chuckles, along with Becca. "I think it's quite miraculous what you're about to see, and I think it will change the way mining here in my beloved state of Wyoming is done. See, I was born and raised in Crystal Lake. I went to college in Cheyenne and earned degrees in environmental studies and public policy. I love this state, and the entire United States. I want a safe, clean way to get energy. I've consulted and worked with multiple state departments, and I've never seen anything like what you're about to see."

She could taste the anticipation in the air, and she needed to get to it. So she decided to skip the last few paragraphs of her speech. "So, without further adieu, let me introduce you to the Whittaker brothers, one of which is the brains and drive behind this project, and the other is the one who ensures that everyone will know about it. First, Andrew Whittaker, the public relations director at Springside Energy."

She stepped to the side and clapped, relieved she'd spoken the last word she needed to and that everyone in front of her started applauding too.

Andrew stepped to her side, full of energy and excitement, perfect for this crowd. "Thank you, Becca. Isn't she great?" He beamed at her, and she thought she saw an edge of adoration in his gaze before she stepped past him and took her seat next to Graham.

She noticed how tightly he had his arms clenched across his chest. Heard the *click click click* of cameras. She leaned over and said, "It's going to be great. You should relax."

He tipped his chin toward her, barely looking at her. But he dropped his hands to his lap and his shoulders released their tension.

"You don't even have to speak," she whispered. "That was terrifying."

"You did great," he whispered, and Becca focused on Andrew at the podium. His speech included a brief history of the company, as well as their current method of mining. They'd pared it down as much as possible, as most people didn't need all the specifics.

During their rehearsals, his speech had been six minutes long. It passed quickly, and Graham stood to lift the screen while she and Andrew and a few others moved their chairs to the side.

The podium got dragged to the side, and Andrew stepped over to the projector he'd set up himself.

The video started, and the crowd hushed. When it was over, Andrew lifted the mic to his mouth. "And that's the SonarBot. We'll take a few questions."

Becca moved to stand beside Andrew, and Graham took his spot on the other side. A beat of silence entered her ears, and then the shouts started.

———

By the time she made it to the silence and safety of her car, Becca never wanted to have another press conference again. She sighed and leaned her head against the rest behind her. The questions hadn't been bad. No one had any reason to protest. There was simply clamoring for more information on the SonarBot, which Andrew and Graham had promised to send to everyone before lunch so they could make their publication deadlines.

Her passenger door opened, and she startled, a yelp squeaking out of her mouth.

"It's just me." Andrew folded himself into the car and closed the door. "Holy cow." He sighed just the way she had and added, "It's hot in here. Are we going to lunch?"

"I just needed a minute." She twisted the key in the ignition and got the air conditioner running. "That was intense."

"And that was our friendliest audience." Andrew rubbed his forehead as if he had an unseen ache there.

"Other crowds will be receptive too," she said. After all, she'd done the metrics on the places they were going. Ran polls to find out about how people felt about fracking and energy companies, noise levels and outsiders coming to their towns. She'd assigned each meeting and tour stop a reception rating, and they weren't all bad.

"You were great," he said. "Threw me for a bit of a loop

when you skipped a bunch of stuff, but great." He took her hand in his, and she looked at him.

"Thanks," she said. "You're the true master in front of a crowd."

He shook his head, such a different man than who'd been on the front steps earlier. And a wildly different one than that cowboy riding his beloved horse. In that moment, Becca decided she liked the cowboy best, because Andrew seemed to be his true self while atop Wolfgang, nothing manufactured between them.

"We'll be late for lunch," he murmured. But he didn't look away from her. "And there are people watching."

Becca nodded like they were having a real conversation about really important things. "Are you going to leave your car here?"

"You can bring me back after lunch," he said. "And then we'll proceed as planned."

Yes, they had a plan for everything, and Becca nodded again. "Lunch it is, then."

She released his hand and put the car in gear, ready to keep pretending she and Andrew were just co-workers for a few more hours. But tonight, after they checked into their rooms, she wanted to curl into his side and listen to him compliment her performance again.

They were two of the last people to arrive in the private room at the steakhouse, and Andrew introduced her to Laney, Bailey, Ronnie, and his mother, as they were the rest of his family she hadn't met.

She shook their hands and giggled at baby Ronnie's flushed face. "He's teething," Laney said, bouncing the drooling baby on her hip. "It's kind of a nightmare." But she smiled in a real way and strapped him in a high chair.

"Oh, you're Andrew's Becca." His mother hugged Becca while she tried to figure out how to respond.

"Mother," Andrew said in a low voice. "She's the press secretary."

Becca caught the growl in his voice though it probably wasn't obvious to anyone else. Well, his mother got it too, because she fell back, her face one of horror. She smoothed it over faster than Andrew could have, and Becca suddenly knew where he'd gotten his skills.

"You both did great this morning," she said. "That's all I meant. It's clear you work well together."

Becca smiled and said, "Nice to meet you," before stepping away and taking her assigned seat at the table. She was positioned right beside the mayor's wife, and she engaged Loretta in a conversation about the upcoming Halloween festival.

She managed to make it through lunch with all her professionalism still in place. But wow, it was exhausting. She needed a respite, a place of refuge, and the one person she'd been using for that these past few weeks was off-limits.

So she rode in the backseat of the car with her legs crossed and a half-dozen folders between her and Andrew. They debriefed that morning's speeches and events, and prepared for the next press conference. And while she was with her boyfriend, she certainly didn't feel like it.

How's it going? Raven's text came at just the right time, because Becca felt like she was going to snap.

What did you think of this morning? she asked.

I meant with you and Andrew.

She cut him a glance out of the corner of her eye, but he was absorbed in a report, probably something he'd read two dozen times.

I don't know if I can do this for three weeks. Becca looked at the typed words, torn between sending them or erasing them and simply saying *Great!*

The job won't always be like this, she told herself. But it did concern her with how easily Andrew slipped from one role to another, and she wondered if he'd been pretending with her at all.

Why else would he still be with you?

The thought sounded in her head in a male voice—Jarom's voice—but that didn't make it any less valid. After all, she'd taken the job at Springside to influence change from the inside. Maybe he had an ulterior motive for hiring her.

She pressed SEND on her text just as her phone buzzed again.

A text from Andrew: *Can't wait to kiss you later.*

She glanced at him, surprised and utterly confused. He chuckled and shoved his phone in the pocket of the seat in front of him.

Becca didn't know what to say back, so she didn't respond. She silenced her phone all the way so she wouldn't even know when it buzzed, dropped it in the pocket on her side of the car, and tried to figure out why she had such self-loathing and how to get over it before she lost a man who seemed genuinely interested in her.

CHAPTER 15

Andrew knocked on Becca's door, a bag of food in his hand. The motions felt so familiar, as did her smile when she opened the door wearing a pair of yoga pants and one of her T-shirts he'd come to love.

"There are a lot of French fries in here." He lifted the bag, and she took it.

"I love you," she said, and he stumbled over the threshold of her room.

"I'm sorry. What?"

"Oh, that was the wrong thing to say?" She exhaled heavily. "I can't talk without a written speech." She gave him a flirty smile. "I meant thank you for the French fries."

He relaxed, because of course she wasn't going to profess her love for him after only three and a half weeks of dating. "We made it through the first day." He let the door close behind him, and then he engaged the deadbolt.

"It was exhausting." She sank onto the loveseat in the small sitting area beside the bed. "I honestly don't know how I'm going to survive the next three weeks."

"I did try to warn you." He sat beside her and lifted his arm over her shoulder, grateful and thrilled when she melted into his side. "I've wanted to hold you like this all day," he murmured, and she tipped her head back to kiss him.

Finally, he thought as a sigh passed through his whole body. He wondered if he was in love with Becca, but he didn't let his thoughts go too far down that path. It was one he hadn't been on in far too long, and he didn't know the dangers.

"I want to tell you something," she said, breaking their connection and sitting up straighter. She pulled a couple of burgers out of the bag to get to the fries.

"All right."

"It's a personal thing." She didn't look at him but busied herself with opening a ketchup packet.

"I'm prepared for personal things."

"I've only had one boyfriend longer than you."

Andrew's heart stumbled over its beat. "We've been dating for less than a month."

"Twenty-four days," she said.

"And that's your second-longest relationship?"

"If we make it through the tour, you'll be the longest." She finally looked at him, and he found vulnerability and something else in her eyes. Something he couldn't identify. "Men don't like me for long, Andrew."

He wasn't sure how that was possible. He studied her, trying to figure out what to say to reassure her that *he* liked her.

In the end, he simply went with, "I like you, Becca."

"I can't figure out why." She did seem genuinely confused, maybe a little sad.

He picked up a burger and started unwrapping it. "Well, you're beautiful, for one. The smartest person I know. Determined to do what you think is right. You're a hard worker. You feed strays. You love your family." He took a bite of the burger, wishing his list wasn't so superficial.

He swallowed. "I like that you came to ride horses with me when you hadn't been on one in years. I like that you ask me hard questions. I like being with you, because you make me feel relaxed." He shrugged, but at least those reasons felt more substantial than *you're pretty*.

She put a few fries in her mouth, but the atmosphere between them felt charged now.

"And for the record," he said, forcing himself to slow down with the consumption of his burger. "I like you more than any other woman I've ever met." His throat felt sticky, like he'd never be able to swallow another bite of food or say another sentence.

"Thank you," she said, and she lifted her burger to unwrap it too.

Andrew wanted to say more, convince her of how he felt, but he didn't know how. He knew better than most that some things had to be worked through on a personal level. Just like he wasn't ready for his mother to start dating again, but she obviously was, and none of his other brothers seemed to have a problem with it.

Even Eli had texted to say *If it makes her happy, I think it's fine.*

Andrew hadn't asked for more details about Admiral and his mom, but they'd gone out several more times over the past few weeks.

"Well, should we go over tomorrow?" Becca asked.

"Yeah." Andrew added a sigh to the end.

"Hey," she said nudging him with her shoulder. "It's only day one."

"I don't like the tour," he admitted, probably for the first time to anyone, even himself. "I feel like I'm...being fake. Like it's all just a show."

Her face lit up and she said, "It's exactly like that. You're really good at it."

"Being fake?" That wasn't what he wanted to be good at. He searched her face and found some truth there. "You think I'm fake." He sat forward on the couch.

"You...have a lot of moving parts."

"Look who's being diplomatic now." He scoffed, but a pinch

of hurt started way down at the bottom of his lungs and worked its way up. "That's all I'm doing, you know."

"I know," she said. "But I can't decide who you are quite yet."

"Who I am?" Andrew knew exactly who he was. "Who do you think I am?"

"Well, there's the Andrew that wears fancy suits and shiny shoes, with never a hair out of place. And he's all business, and everyone listens to him."

Andrew's heart raced listening to her. Was that how everyone saw him? He did work to make sure he was professional when he arrived at work. "Am I intimidating?"

"Not to me," she said. "But I see you with your tie loosened, half-asleep on my couch, that tiny spicy chicken breath wafting all over me." She grinned at him, and Andrew scoffed though he liked the way she teased him.

"You liked that tiny spicy chicken breath," he said, slipping his hands around her waist and leaning over her.

She giggled and pushed against his chest fruitlessly. "Stop it," she said, laughing fully between the words.

"Is my tie loose enough for you?" He unknotted it further, pulling it completely from around his neck. She stopped squirming and looked right into his eyes, her hands coming up to touch his neck. She trailed them along the collar of his shirt, sobering the moment further.

"And then there's the cowboy version of you," she whispered, moving her hand to his face in the most intimate gesture Andrew had experienced. He wanted to lock time on this moment forever, this softness between them perfect.

"I like him the best," she said, her eyes dropping to look at his mouth.

"Yeah?" he asked. "Why do you like him the best?"

"Because he seems the most real." Her gaze came back to his, and Andrew pressed his lips to hers, enjoying the way she cradled his face and kissed him back like he was wearing that denim shirt and cowboy hat right now.

And dang, if he didn't want to be a cowboy for her. Every day of the week, at all hours. He let himself kiss her for several long moments, and then he pulled away and sat up again, every cell in his body supercharged and wondering if maybe he'd fallen in love with Becca and didn't know it yet.

She sat up and straightened her hair before reaching to extract a folder from her briefcase bag. Smoothing it on the table, she said, "Tomorrow we're in Star Valley, then Kemmerer, where we're spending the night. The next day we hit Evanston, and then it's a straight shot for days down the interstate to Laramie and Cheyenne."

"It'll be a small crowd in Star Valley," he said. "We don't dig much there, and it's a small population."

"Yes, but their reception rating is a nine." She showed him a paper he barely looked at. "Kemmerer is a six, and we'll be lucky if the questions stop before an hour has passed."

"Lots of drilling in the towns north of there," he said. "We expect the people to come down the road for the meeting, since we aren't going up into the Boulder area."

"And then once we head north again from Cheyenne, the reception ratings go way down again." She shuffled some papers he'd looked at dozens of times. Exhaustion hit him hard, especially now that he'd eaten something and then held Becca in his arms.

"I'm going to head to bed," he said. "I didn't sleep much last night."

"Okay," she said, still looking over something from her folder. Andrew took another long look at her from his position in the doorway, then he unlocked the deadbolt and stepped quickly into the hall. His room was down a few doors, and he went inside and removed his jacket, his shoes, and his belt before the door had even swung closed behind him.

As tired as he was, he still took time to offer his nightly

prayers as well as spend a few minutes thinking about Becca and the depth of his feelings for her. He couldn't quite find the bottom, and he didn't know what that meant.

———

THERE WERE NO SURPRISES IN STAR VALLEY, NOR KEMMERER. THE crowds there were four times as big as Coral Canyon or Star Valley, and the questions did come for quite a long time. But the people simply wanted to know.

Every time Andrew felt his patience waning, Becca would answer questions for a while, the slight touch of her elbow against his a constant reminder to keep his diplomatic face on. She showed up at his door with two boxes of pizza that night, a pair of flip flops in place of her heels and those yoga pants and T-shirt as sexy as the dark-colored dresses and skirts she wore to stand at podiums and make speeches.

"One of those better have olives on it," he said, eyeing the boxes in her hand.

"I got a supreme, Mister Picky Pants." She grinned at him, and he stepped back to let her in. "Olives and green peppers and mushrooms, along with all those meats you like." She set the boxes on the little table in front of the even smaller couch in his hotel room.

She drew in a breath and turned to him, and he swept her into his arms, his mouth already searching for hers. "Spending all day with you and pretending is really hard," he said, his lips touching hers again.

She only answered him by kissing him back.

The tour continued, and honestly, most of it became a blur for Andrew. When the second week started in Laramie, Andrew hoped these bigger crowds would be as receptive to their presentation as the more rural areas had been.

Their biggest challenge was those smaller cities, but some of the big stops along the interstate had drawn some of them down.

Becca had constantly been checking the online polls she'd sent to those towns, and the numbers of interested people were dropping.

"I honestly think it's because they're coming to our other meetings," she said. "I'm not changing the reception ratings."

"Fine, don't change them," he said, playing a game on his phone. He found he really needed some downtime in the evenings. No conversation. No plans. No kissing. Just blind staring as he tried to line up three fruits in a row.

"The mayor of Denver has requested we come there."

That got Andrew's attention, as did the excitement in his girl-friend's voice. "Denver?"

"There are twice as many natural gas drilling sites from Cheyenne to Denver as there are in almost the whole state of Wyoming."

"They don't all use fracking," he said. "And they're not all ours."

"So we're not going to sell SonarBot?"

"No," Andrew said slowly. "SonarBot is ours. It's Graham's. We're not selling it or the technology behind it."

"It's sonar."

"It's a lot more than that," Andrew said, tilting his head. "We can do a presentation for them, but not until the New Year." Just the thought of packing another bag after this tour…yeah, that wasn't happening.

"And even then, it'll just be a basic, this is what we'll be using at our drill sites." Andrew closed his game and set his phone aside. "Now, if we get control of some of the drill sites in Denver—or anywhere else for that matter—then we'll use the SonarBot there."

"So how many will there be?"

"*You* answered this question at the last meeting." He smiled and stood. "Come on. Let's go get something to eat. I'm tired of eating on a tiny couch."

"All right," she said. "But I'm bringing the folder for tomorrow's agenda. Laramie will be our biggest crowd yet."

"If only my family could see you now," he said.

"What does that mean?" she asked, shrugging into her jacket.

"It means they've told me I work more than any person alive, but girlfriend, that's you."

She laughed, and latched onto him. "I like it when you call me your girlfriend."

Andrew liked it too, and he felt himself slipping a little further in love with the beautiful Becca Collings, sure she'd stolen his heart while he was asleep.

CHAPTER 16

Becca pressed her elbow into Andrew's, wishing the man at the microphone would take a breath so she could interrupt. But he had lungs of iron, and her patience with his complaints was going to run out before his air.

Andrew kept his arm solidly on the table too, and she didn't have to look at him to know he was irked too.

"Sir," Becca said, but the man barely flicked his eyes in her direction. He seemed to only want to hear another male speak, but when he finished, Andrew remained as tight-lipped as a clam.

"Sir," Becca said again. "Your concern over the noise will be nearly solved with the introduction of the SonarBot. The decibels it emits are well within city and town ordinances for all of our mines." She did know how to take a breath so she'd sound professional and polite though she wanted to lunge across the table and make that man move back. The line behind him at the mic was easily twelve people long and they'd been answering questions for an hour already.

Becca really was quite tired of it all. Sure, she enjoyed seeing what color Andrew's tie would be, because he never wore the same one. She liked seeing what he'd find in that town they could both enjoy for dinner. She'd learned a lot about his eating habits being on tour with him, and if he didn't get a hot breakfast, someone would probably lose their head by ten a.m.

He'd learned not to put onions on her burgers, and nothing but pepperoni and sausage on her pizza. She could order his coffee with perfection, no matter which shop they stopped at, and he could do the same for her.

By the beginning of the third week of the tour, Becca had reached another milestone in her life. She and Andrew had been dating for forty days, and that was one day longer than her relationship with Jarom.

She didn't say anything to Andrew, because she didn't want to jinx anything. The tour was tiring, that was for sure, but she hadn't hated it.

Until tonight. She'd pegged these mining towns north of Cheyenne exactly right, and this meeting they were currently conducting had a crowd receptive rating at three.

In Becca's opinion, she should've given them a one, because every person who stepped up to speak was negative. Not only that, they didn't seem to have listened to a single thing she or Andrew had said in the presentation.

"What about our jobs?" someone asked, and Becca refrained from rolling her eyes.

"No jobs will be affected by the introduction of the Sonar-Bot," she said, working hard not to speak in a dry monotone. "If anything, we'll need more people to run the robot, interpret the findings, and make decisions for the crew."

The woman stepped away, and someone else moved up to the microphone. "Will there be certain hours for the sonar to be used?"

"Business hours," Andrew said into the mic in front of him. "I'm sorry folks, we only have time for three more questions."

Relief sighed through Becca's whole body, and she let him answer the rest of the questions. They stood and followed a couple of local cops out the front of the gymnasium, where their meeting had been held.

She exited the building to find darkness had claimed the day. Quite a while ago too, if the depth of blackness surrounding her was any indication. She took in a deep breath, enjoying the fresh air out here in the more wild parts of her home state.

"Well, that could've gone better," he grumbled. They hadn't eaten for hours, and Becca understood his foul mood.

"But we did it."

"Three more days," he said as he started for the car.

Glinting lights across the street caught Becca's eye. A church, with the front doors flung wide open.

"Andrew," she said. He turned back to her and she pointed to the church. "Will you wait for me?"

"I'll come with," he said. He spoke to the driver momentarily, and they crossed the street together. She wanted to reach over and slip her hand into his, lean into him and giggle. Well, maybe not giggle. She was so tired she wasn't up for giggling.

They climbed the several steps to the doors of the church and then hesitated. Singing came from inside, and she entered first and moved through the lobby and into the chapel, taking a seat on the very back row.

A choir stood up on the dais at the front, and though they didn't wear their robes, they sang with the voices of angels. Becca's weary soul was immediately soothed, further sighing in comfort and peace when Andrew joined her on the end of the bench.

They simply sat there and listened while the singers practiced their songs, while the director gave corrections, and as Becca's heart filled. She could make it through the next three days. She could.

The call of her own home, her bed and puffy comforter, and her dog had never been so loud, but somehow the choir had drowned it out.

Andrew's phone buzzed, and she glanced at him. "Be right

back," he whispered, sweeping a kiss along her forehead as he stood and left. "Hey," she heard him say when he reached the lobby only a few steps away.

She stayed for another song, and then choir practice started to break up. She felt like perhaps she shouldn't be caught in the back row, so she got to her feet. They protested against her heels, but she managed to tiptoe out into the lobby without anyone shouting for her to come back.

Andrew sat on the front steps, his phone still at his ear. With the country stillness and the choir being finished, she could hear him quite clearly.

"I'm sure that's not true," he said.

Becca paused, not wanting to interrupt him, but not wanting to eavesdrop either. She hadn't caught the name on the screen, and it didn't sound like one of his brothers.

"Dwight, it's simply not true. Can you imagine anyone being attracted to Becca Collings?"

His voice struck her like a thousand-pound weight in the chest.

"I don't care what someone thinks they saw. I'm not dating Becca." He added a chuckle as if such an idea was utterly ridiculous. And Becca just stood there and listened, his words sinking way down deep into the soul that moments ago had felt whole.

This was far worse than anything Jarom had said to her, and Andrew stabbed a knife right into her pounding heart with, "She's literally one of the most annoying women on the planet. I can't imagine anyone liking her for long."

A squeak escaped from her lips, and Andrew twisted toward her. He shot to his feet, his eyes wide. "I have to go, Dwight. I'll call you later."

By the time Andrew finished speaking, Becca had flown past him and was all the way down the steps. "Becca," he called after her, but a tornado churned inside her, and she couldn't trust herself to turn back to him and have a conversation right now.

"Can I ride in the front please?" she asked the driver, yanking open the door before he even answered. She sniffed, her tears brimming against her eyelids. She swiped at them quickly, before Andrew could see her.

"Becca." He slid into the backseat as the driver rounded the front of the car.

"I don't want to talk about it." She eyed the driver. "Right now. Please."

Andrew leaned back into his seat, pure resignation on his face. Becca folded her arms and stared out the passenger window, willing the miles to the hotel to pass quickly. They hadn't even checked in yet, and she stood several paces behind him while he took care of everything. He'd always taken care of these arrangements, but she'd stood right next to him, accepted her key, and waited to make arrangements for dinner.

Tonight, she could barely hold back the tears.

I can't imagine anyone liking her for long. She'd told him that men didn't like her for very long, and he'd gone on to list all the things he liked about her. Whenever she had a moment of self-doubt, she repeated that list until she believed another one.

He turned from the check-in desk, but he didn't extend her key to her. A tear splashed her cheek, and she wiped it away furiously. She would not cry in front of him. She lifted her chin instead, reciting how to spell great big words so she could focus on the letters instead of letting her emotions control her.

"Becca," he said for a third time, and she held out her hand.

He took a few steps toward her. "Are we going to talk about it? It was Dwight. I had to say something."

It had sounded so true, and Becca wasn't sure how she could get such horrible words out of her ears. She'd given him more of herself than anyone else, and she'd genuinely started to believe that perhaps Andrew would never break up with her.

"I need a few minutes," she whispered. "Can I please have my key?" She shook her hand impatiently, like she would for a disobedient child who hadn't passed over something she'd requested.

He handed her a small envelope. "Room four-eleven."

She spun away from him and snatched her bag on her way to the elevator. He let her go, and she half-wanted him to come with her, ride up to the fourth floor, and apologize again.

Wait, he hadn't apologized at all yet.

Anger filled Becca, and she marched down the hall to her room, realizing she was going to need a lot longer than a few minutes to sort through her feelings.

As soon as the door closed behind her, she pressed her back into it and let the tears fall.

————

"Great, thank you Mayor Berry. I'll be by on Monday morning. Thank you." She hung up before she could gush out another declaration of gratitude.

She was twenty minutes late for her morning meeting with Andrew, and while that fact gnawed at her, she also had some things to take care of. Her phone rang again, and this time it was Andrew.

"I'm coming," she said after answering the phone. "Be down in two minutes." After zipping her bag closed, she made one quick glance around the room to make sure she got her charger and earrings from the night table.

She had refused to let Andrew come by the previous evening, instead claiming that she was simply too tired and nothing good could come from the conversation until morning.

But instead of sleeping and getting the rest she desperately needed, Becca had spent a couple of hours looking at the online job boards in Wyoming. She wasn't sure how she was even going to survive the next three days with Andrew, let alone working on the other side of the wall from him indefinitely.

It was Dwight. I had to say something.

Yes, she thought as she left her room, her bag behind her.

"But he didn't have to use the exact thing I told him in confidence. That I'm obviously sensitive about."

He paced in the lobby, his phone pressed to his ear, and when his eye caught hers, he looked part relieved, part sorry, and mostly irritated.

She didn't apologize. After all, he hadn't. And she'd needed to make the call to the Mayor's office in Coral Canyon to see if he could use her. And as it turned out, he wanted to talk. So she'd be as late as she wanted, thank you very much.

He hung up and faced her. "Ready?"

Becca nodded, wishing her voice hadn't abandoned her. She walked a half-step behind him as they went outside and got in their car. While the driver loaded her bag in the trunk, she scooted all the way against the door and folded her arms. She had something very important to say to him, and she wanted to do it in private. But as soon as the driver got in, they wouldn't be alone again for the rest of the day.

Andrew could handle news like this, as he was really very talented at acting like everything was wonderful when it wasn't. Heck, he'd probably been pretending in his feelings for her all this time.

The driver approached his door, and Becca said, "Andrew, consider this my two weeks notice."

CHAPTER 17

A ndrew woke on Saturday morning to sunshine streaming through his window. For a moment, he didn't know where he was. He'd been waking to the sound of an alarm, and only letting the sun in once he opened the blackout curtains in his hotel room.

But the tour had ended yesterday. He'd returned to the lodge about mid-afternoon and gone in his bedroom. He hadn't come out once, and surely Celia would've rallied everyone in the family by now.

He didn't care. He needed all the help he could get. Because Becca wouldn't talk to him, and she'd given her notice that she was quitting.

"She can't quit," he said, just like he had about ten other times in the past three days. But he didn't know how to get her to stay. She'd been so good at dealing with difficult conversations when they didn't involve her.

But now, she'd basically shut him out. He had ways of learning things though, and he knew she had a meeting with Mayor Berry on Monday morning. He'd told her to take a few days off, but that was over a week ago, before she'd heard him call her annoying and that no one could possibly stand her for very long.

His chest tightened, and tightened until he felt sure a rib would crack. Why had he said those things? Dwight had called because someone had been talking about him and Becca online. They claimed to have a picture of them kissing, but Andrew knew that simply wasn't true. He'd only kissed Becca in one of their hotel rooms, and there wasn't anyone around to see that.

So he'd denied it.

"Lied about it," he muttered to himself, though he'd always known he'd have to deny the relationship if someone brought it up.

He looked like the living dead, and his hair stood up at odd angles. He didn't care. He cracked his bedroom door and listened to see if anyone was in the kitchen. He couldn't hear anything, so he went down the hall, past the empty office, and into the vacant kitchen. He knew how to make coffee, despite everyone's assumptions, and he got a pot going while he hunted around for a loaf of bread.

With a stack of toast and a cup of coffee, Andrew stepped into the backyard. He didn't know where Bree was at the moment, but she'd obviously been hard at work on the grounds. The trees had all been trimmed back. The rose bushes too. Grape vines. Everything had been clipped and rounded and readied for the oncoming winter.

Andrew was actually surprised it hadn't snowed in Coral Canyon yet. The Tetons always had snow on them, but he expected the weather to turn any day now.

"I can't believe I'm standing here thinking about the weather." He wandered down the sidewalk a little bit, finishing his toast as he went to the stables.

Someone was inside when he entered, and his first instinct was to leave. He didn't want to see anyone, and he certainly didn't want them to see him. Becca had said the cowboy version of him was her favorite, because he was the most real.

He wondered what she'd think of him now, in gym shorts and a T-shirt, hair a mess, and unshaven for the past three days.

Jake worked in the stables, and when he saw Andrew, his face burst into a grin. "Hey, there, Andrew," he said, coming down the aisle to shake Andrew's hand. "You're back in town then?"

"Yeah, back in town." Andrew really wanted to be back on tour—at least the first two and a half weeks, when Becca was talking to him, kissing him, soothing him.

"So you want me to go back to just evenings?"

Andrew didn't know what he wanted. "Let's keep the schedule for now, Jake."

"Sure thing."

"Thanks." Andrew finished his coffee and moved down to Wolfgang's stall. "Hey, bud." The horse seemed to remember him, and he didn't ask any questions about schedules or women or anything else Andrew didn't know how to answer.

"I'll come back this afternoon and we'll go for a ride, okay?"

Wolfgang nickered as if he understood English, and Andrew smiled at the gentle horse. "What am I going to do about Becca?" he whispered so Jake couldn't hear him. "She won't even talk to me." He'd never felt so heartbroken before, and he never thought he would.

Becca had changed his life in more ways than one, and he wasn't sure how he could survive even a single day without her.

But survive he did. Celia had left food in the fridge, so he had plenty to eat. He spent a couple of hours on Wolfgang's back. Then he retreated to his bedroom and put something on his tablet he simply stared at.

Sunday morning dawned, and Graham texted to find out if Andrew wanted a ride to church. Andrew hesitated, thinking of the last time he'd been in a chapel. Not only that, but Graham and Laney would take one look at him and want to know what had happened on tour.

Andrew looked into his own eyes and hardly recognized

himself. Did he have so many sides that even he didn't know them all?

I'm too tired, he sent to his brother, and he stepped into the shower so he couldn't engage in any argument that might come from Graham. He should be glad he didn't have to drive the minivan.

Andrew skipped shaving for another day, thinking maybe he'd grow a beard again now that the tour was over. Maybe then he'd know who he wanted to be, as if such a thing could be determined by something as simple as facial hair.

————

HE DIDN'T GO INTO THE OFFICE FOR A WEEK, AND THAT WAS A NEW record for him. He felt somewhat like a hermit, as he avoided Celia and Bree when they were in the house, and spent all his time with the horses or by himself.

He'd tried calling Becca exactly once, and she'd answered with, "Andrew, I don't think this is going to work out. I'm sorry."

She was sorry? He hadn't known what to say, and she'd said, "Good-bye, Andrew," meaning more than the phone call.

His heart felt like someone had taken it out of his chest, shattered it on the ground, and then tried to put all the shards back together. He honestly hadn't known it was possible to develop such strong feelings for someone in such a short time.

But he now knew he was capable of falling for someone. But he wasn't in love with her. Oh, no. Maybe he could've gotten there, had he gotten a bit more time with her.

The day before Halloween, Carla called and asked if he was coming in the next day, as there was a building-wide party and each department competed for the best costumes. He didn't want to ask if Becca would be there, but the department usually dressed in a theme and entered the competition together.

"And so you know, Becca cleaned out her office. She said she'd finish the final reports at home, and her last paycheck could be mailed."

Andrew heard the tentativeness in her voice and knew she wanted more details. "Thank you," he said. "Yes, I'll be in tomorrow. What should we do?" Now that their department was down to two, it shouldn't be too hard.

"I was thinking," she said. "Your family has a Santa suit, don't they?"

"Yes," Andrew said, suddenly reminded of the upcoming Christmas holidays—and how all of his plans had included Becca.

Andrew made it through three days at work before Graham and Beau showed up in his office.

"Hey," he said, surprise coloring the word. He leaned away from the paperwork on his desk. "What's going on?"

Graham looked grim, and he entered the office and closed the door behind him. "This is an intervention."

Andrew scoffed and started to smile when he realized his brothers weren't kidding. "An intervention for what?"

Beau removed his cowboy hat and ran his free hand through his hair. "You and Becca Collings."

"There is no me and Becca Collings," Andrew said, his tone dark now.

"I told him you two were, in fact, dating." Graham took a chair across from Andrew, not a hint of regret in his face or his voice.

"Great." Andrew waited, thinking if they said what they'd come to say, they'd leave.

"What happened?" Graham asked as Beau dragged over a chair and sat beside him.

"We weren't compatible."

Beau laughed, and Graham simply smiled. "We know that's not true," his oldest brother said.

"I did something stupid, and she's mad at me," he said, realizing as he spoke that no, she wasn't mad. She was hurt. He'd said horrible, mean things, even if they weren't true.

"Have you tried talking to her?" Graham asked.

"Yes," Andrew said. "She won't."

"And that's okay with you? The Andrew Whittaker I know doesn't just let someone avoid him." Beau exchanged a glance with Graham. "Remember when he ran for senior class president and he needed more votes? He went house to house, passing out little candies and asking people to vote for him."

"I did not."

"I do remember that," Graham said. "And he won too."

"I'm sitting right here."

"Look," Graham said, leaning forward. "If you like this woman, and I think you do based on what I'm seeing in front of me, you go talk to her."

"Yeah, the beard's nice," Beau said with a smile that said it really wasn't all that nice. "And I like how you're letting your hair grow out."

"Shut it," Andrew said.

"C'mon, Beau. Let's go grab lunch."

"Am I not invited?" Andrew stood, thinking lunch with his brothers was just what he needed.

"I'm sorry." Graham cocked his head. "Did you hear something?"

"No, I don't think I did." Beau opened the door and walked out, leaving Andrew fuming in his office.

"I know you can hear me," he called after them.

Graham came back and said, "Go talk to her."

Andrew flexed his fists and waited until his brother was out of earshot. "Easy for you to say," he muttered, though he'd heard the stories of how Graham had gone to Laney and they'd talked through what was keeping them apart.

But Andrew didn't think simply showing up at Becca's with

a pepperoni and sausage pizza, an apology, and a smile would be enough.

Problem was, Andrew didn't think he'd make it through the holidays without her. And he had no other ideas for how to get her back. He only knew he had to try.

CHAPTER 18

Becca went through the motions of feeding Otto and filling the bowls on her back patio. With winter coming, the level of dread over keeping the food and water available for the strays had risen.

In fact, everything made her cranky lately. Or sad. Or desperate. Nothing in her life was the same without Andrew, and the sight of the clothes she'd bought on his company's credit card mocked her from their hangers in her closet.

Worse was when she had to wear something from that collection to her new job at the Mayor's office. She hated this job, but it did pay well, and she did need the income. Or maybe she just needed something to occupy her time, keep her busy so she wouldn't be able to spend hours thinking about Andrew and what he was doing at Springside.

She kept her eye on the news so she'd know when the first SonarBots went out in the field, as she had personally promised the media and the Mayor that they'd be the first to know. In fact, they were supposed to be able to be on-site when it sent its first sonar emissions into the rocks.

But a week passed, then two, and finally three and nothing hit the headlines. Maybe there had been a complication. Maybe with the worsening weather, Andrew had decided to wait until spring to try the new technology. They'd spoken of that once, briefly, when the timelines to SonarBot usage had been outlined.

She missed her meetings in Andrew's office, the sly touch of his hand on hers when they exchanged a folder. The quick glances that promised dinner—and kissing—later.

Someone set something on her desk, jolting her out of her memories. Or maybe her misery. She looked up into Raven's eyes.

"You missed lunch." Her best friend wore a look of concern mixed with compassion. "I called you three times."

Becca turned over her phone, which was on silent. She didn't even know what time it was, but she saw now that it was almost one-thirty, and she was supposed to meet Raven an hour ago.

Guilt filled her, and her shoulders slumped. "I'm sorry, Raven."

"It's fine. I brought you the barbecue chicken salad." Raven sat in the empty desk beside Becca's. "When are you going to call him and tell him you made a mistake?"

Raven opened the Styrofoam container to lettuce, tomato, bacon, cheese, and all that delicious grilled barbecue chicken. "I'm not going to call him. We aren't meant to be."

Raven snorted, but Becca ignored her. "You're delusional."

"Why? Because I've been proven right once again? Men don't stick around for long, and he's one of the best men—" Her voice choked and she cut herself off.

"You guys were great together. I'm sure he's miserable too." Raven covered Becca's hand with one of her own. "It's obvious you still love him."

Love him? Becca snorted and started laughing. "I'm not in love with him." She was terribly lonely at night, that was for sure. She had no passion for this job. And she just wanted to eat her salad and go back to reading...whatever she was supposed to be reading.

Raven stood. "Well, I have to get back to work, but I think you should call him."

He'd called her once, and she hadn't even answered with a hello. Of course, he had yet to apologize for calling her one of the most annoying women on the planet, or insinuating that no one could like her for long.

She tried to push the insults out of her mind, but they never went far. And today, as Raven patted her hand once more and left, the things Andrew had said—whether to get his general manager off his back or not—shouted through her mind.

She pushed the chicken salad away, though it was one of her favorite foods. She had no appetite anymore, as Andrew seemed to infect every aspect of her life.

She didn't remember feeling this way after Jarom had broken up with her. Or anyone else for that matter, probably because none of those dates had ever really turned into a relationship.

But Becca knew that everything had its opposite. Light and darkness. Pleasure and pain. She thought she'd known the opposite of joy was misery, but she hadn't. Not until now.

Now, she knew what true misery felt like, and she couldn't help but wonder if she'd experienced true joy when she was with Andrew. And now that she wasn't....

She reached for her phone and texted Raven. *How do I just call him? What do I even say?*

You say, I love you. I'm sorry. Want to bring me dinner? Raven included a smiley face emoji with her text, and Becca wondered if she could just copy and paste her text into a new message for Andrew.

"Becca?" Mayor Berry stood at her desk, and Becca jerked to attention, stumbling as she stood.

"Yes, sir."

"Why didn't we get notice about the SonarBot?"

Confusion rushed through her. "What are you talking about?"

He pointed to the television in the corner, which played

constantly, the sound muted. The screen showed the SonarBot rumbling along the rocks, with the newscaster's head in the top right corner. The captions, though delayed, got the message across just fine.

"...this inauguration of the single most advanced piece of technology to come to the mining industry ever."

"Turn it up," she said, navigating through the maze of desks. She reached the TV and dragged a chair underneath it, pressing the volume button so they could hear in real time.

Andrew's face came on the screen, and he wore a smile the size of Texas. It was so fake, Becca wanted to scoff in disgust, as she'd done before. But now she knew the man behind that false grin, knew how much it hurt him to put it on his face, and knew how tired it made him.

"It's a great day," he said, as if he'd won a million dollars. "I can't wait to see the SonarBot in action." But he'd already seen it.

The camera panned to include Graham, who wore a look of happiness and anxiety, and Becca wished she'd had more time to get to know Andrew's family. She felt like she would've fit in great with them.

The interviews continued, even as the Mayor's office started getting dozens of phone calls.

"I don't know," she said to Mayor Berry. "Andrew didn't call you?"

"No," he said, his powerful features crunched in confusion. And anger. "He said—*you* said you guys would call."

"I don't work there anymore." Obviously. But she still wanted to stand by all her promises.

"Where are they?" he asked an advisor who approached with a phone at each ear. "Can I make it in time?"

"They're way over in Douglas," the man said. "I have the chopper pilot on the line. He says he can get us there in a couple of hours."

The Mayor looked at the television, frustration and fury on his face. "We won't make it." He turned away. "Get me Andrew

Whittaker on the phone as soon as possible." He stormed into his office and slammed the door. Becca flinched, feeling the reverberation all the way down in her stomach.

Andrew had broken his promise. Why?

Not only had he alienated the mayor of his own town, but he'd broken the trust he'd worked to achieve. And he'd made her look bad too.

He has to have a good reason, she thought. But she couldn't think of one. In fact, her brain could hardly come up with solutions at all.

She pulled out her phone and called his office, knowing he wasn't there. "Hello, Andrew Whittaker's office," Carla said.

"Hello," she said. "Is Andrew in?"

"I'm afraid not." Carla actually sounded sorry about it too. "May I take a message for him?"

"This is Becca," she said, almost adding "from the mayor's office," but she pulled those words back. "I'm wondering when he'll be back in town."

"Oh, Becca." Carla sounded a bit surprised. "He's scheduled to be back the day after tomorrow."

"Thank you, Carla."

"Do you want to meet with him?"

Desperately, Becca thought but again kept silent. "Mayor Berry would like to, but I'm still working on his availability."

"Well, let me know, hon. I—the office isn't the same without you here."

Becca almost hung up, but something in Carla's tone made her pause. "What do you mean? I was only there a few weeks."

"And Andrew calmed right down," Carla said. "He's back to the highly anxious man he was before you showed up."

"I'm sorry," Becca said, wishing she didn't apologize for things that weren't her fault. "It was a tough job for me."

"I understand. Maybe we could still go to lunch?"

"Sure, Carla. Anytime." She did end the call then, and she

wished she could go waltzing into the cafeteria at Springside and eat with Carla. She'd even wear heels if she had to.

Her chest pinched, but she had one more phone call to make. He was obviously still busy, but he owed the mayor an explanation.

She expected the call to go to his voicemail on the first ring, as he never kept his phone on when he was expecting to be on camera or speaking to a crowd. She stared at his face on the TV while she said, "Andrew, I'm looking at you while the SonarBot is gearing up to send a pulse into the rocks outside Douglas. Mayor Berry is wondering why he was not invited, and frankly, so am I. Please call me back at your earliest convenience."

She hung up, a smile on her face for the first time in weeks.

CHAPTER 19

Andrew hadn't listened to the message on his phone yet. It could be from one of three people, one of whom was Becca.

She'd called.

Why had she called?

He sat in his own hotel room, the room service cart over in the corner, the food subpar at this tiny spot in Douglas. If Becca had been with him, he'd be in her room, probably a couple of pizza boxes on the table in front of them.

He hadn't told her about the first SonarBot expedition. He hadn't told anyone, because he was barely functioning these days.

It had been quite a fail anyway. Sure, the robot had sent its sonar pulses into the rocks, but it hadn't detected any gas. So it was all quite anti-climatic. Sort of like sitting there in his room, wondering if the message would be from Carla, his mom, or Becca.

They'd all called that afternoon.

He hit the button to listen to his voicemail and learned he had three messages. His mother wanted to let him know that she'd ended things with Admiral, and oh, Beau was hosting

Thanksgiving dinner at his bachelor pad because of his new case.

Andrew wasn't sure what a case had to do with where Beau ate, but Andrew wasn't going to argue. Celia would make all the food anyway, except maybe the pies his mother would be responsible for.

Carla said, "Becca called, sir. I think you should call her when you get back."

He wanted to call her right now. If he did, would she tell him to get lost? Report him to the police for continuing contact with her when she'd asked him to stop?

Her voice came on the message next, and his heart leapt around inside his chest like a frog. She sounded stern during the message, all until she said, "Please call me back at your earliest convenience."

Andrew almost sobbed as he started laughing. Sure, she was still mad at him, because he had promised Mayor Berry he'd have a front-row seat to the SonarBot's first excursion. And Becca? Becca should be at his side. At work. At home. Always.

He'd wanted to invite her to do everything with him since the tour ended three weeks ago. But she'd made it very clear she wasn't interested. Could she still be interested? He listened to her message again, definitely detecting a note of playfulness in her last sentence.

Graham's admonition from last week still rang in Andrew's ears, but he didn't know how to show up at Becca's unannounced and talk to her.

But she had asked him to call her. Could he simply do that? Would it really be that easy?

He touched the phone icon and pulled up her name. Another tap and the phone started opening a connection. Maybe it would be this easy.

Her line rang and rang, and she didn't answer. "Hey," he said to her messages. "It's my earliest convenience, and I'm returning your call. I'll be honest and say I completely forgot about letting Mayor Berry know about the SonarBot."

He paused. He forgot, because *she* had been handling all those details.

"And I miss you. I'll be back in town in a couple of days. Maybe we can get together then?"

He had so much more to say, but he didn't want to fill her voicemail with desperate pleas for her to give him another chance. So he finished with, "All right. Talk to you later," and hung up, hoping later came sooner than three weeks without talking to her.

Twenty minutes later, he was still staring at the TV, no idea which channel he'd even put it on. His phone rang, and he glanced down, his eyesight a bit blurry.

But he still saw Becca's name and hurried to answer the call. "Hey," he said, trying not to breathe her name out like he was in love with her.

All at once, he realized he was in love with her.

He'd never had a chance to ask her about his father, and he didn't even care. He *loved* her.

His heart started pounding and he pulled in a tight breath. "Hello?"

"Hey," she said. "Sorry, I was outside bringing in all the cat bowls. Or dog bowls. Raccoon bowls." She blew out her breath as if she'd been running a marathon. "It's snowing pretty hard. I left my phone inside. You called?"

"You called me. I was just returning at my earliest convenience."

A beat of silence passed, and then she said, "Mayor Berry was pretty angry. Have you talked to him?"

"No." Andrew sighed. "I'll call him."

"His advisor should've called and left a message."

"Well, he didn't." Was she accusing him of something? He had three messages after the SonarBot had failed to find any natural gas. None of them had been from the mayor's advisor. "Aren't *you* the mayor's advisor?"

"In a way," she said evasively, which meant, in Becca-speak, no. Andrew wondered what she was doing there, but he was smart enough not to ask.

"I told him I'd find out why you didn't bother to call him to witness the first SonarBot expedition."

Andrew pinched the bridge of his nose, foolishness filling him from top to bottom. She hadn't called because she missed him and wanted to hear his voice. She'd called because it was her job to call. The joke had just been...what? A joke, perhaps.

"I didn't read your notes," he said, going for the truth. "I dropped the ball. I forgot."

"When's the next one?" she asked.

"I don't know. Did you watch the whole thing?"

She coughed, a fake sound he'd heard many times when she was about to admit something she wasn't proud of. He imagined her lifting her chin too. "No."

"Well, it was a fail," he said. "So tell him not to get all bent out of shape. Graham's going to do some tweaks and run some tests, and we'll do another live excursion. I won't forget to invite him."

Or you, he wanted to add but kept way down deep in his gut.

"Thank you," she said.

He hated this diplomatic game they were playing. He knew the rules, knew the outcome, and he hated it.

"Well, thanks for calling."

"Did you listen to my message?" he asked.

"No, I just saw you called."

So she hadn't heard him admit that he missed her. Hadn't listened to him ask her out again when he got back to town. Maybe he could convince her to delete it without listening, just to save some pride.

"It just said I forgot. You can delete it."

"Okay."

"Okay," he echoed. But neither one of them hung up. On her end of the line, a dog barked and she exclaimed, "Oh!" and said, "I have to go, Andrew. I'll call you later."

A second later, the line was dead. Closed. She was gone.

Andrew let his hand holding his phone fall to his lap. How was he going to survive the holidays without her?

———

THANKSGIVING MORNING FOUND HIM IN THE KITCHEN WITH CELIA, adding chopped celery, onions, and carrots to a pan sizzling with butter.

"Stir those around." She handed him a wooden spoon.

"I'm going to burn them," he said.

"Just stir them." She returned to the huge loaf of bread she'd made a few days ago and refused to let him have even one slice. She used a large knife to cut the loaf into cubes for the stuffing, and then she stepped back over to him with a small, glass bowl in her hand. "Add this."

He dumped in the spices and went back to stirring. She'd confronted him last night and practically demanded he get up and help her this morning. She'd said, "You can't hide out in that bedroom forever."

"I'm not hiding," he'd said. "There isn't anyone to hide from here."

She'd made a grumpy noise and said, "Seven o'clock. We're starting the stuffing. Then we'll make a chocolate pie, the yams, and prepare the creamed corn. We have to leave at eleven to get to Beau's and get everything hot again."

He'd watched her march away, down the hall and up the stairs to the room she slept in when she stayed at the lodge.

The scent of sage and garlic wafted up from the pan, and Andrew kept the wooden spoon moving so he didn't char anything.

Celia took over once the vegetables were soft and a bit see-through. She mixed in some chicken stock and added the panfull of ingredients to the big bowl of bread cubes. The stuffing got smashed in a pan and put in the oven, and she turned to him.

"Want to separate eggs or peel yams?"

"Peel yams." He felt sure his clumsy fingers would break the yolk of an egg if he tried to separate it from its white. She set him in front of the sink, which was filled with the knobbly, brown-skinned yams. He started peeling, his bicep muscle complaining after one yam had been skinned.

But he kept on, because Celia wasn't pestering him with questions and he wanted to contribute to the family meal some-how. By eleven, he'd showered and shaved and pulled his sedan right up into the circle drive at the lodge. It was covered, and Mother Nature had decided that snow on Thanksgiving would be beneficial.

With the backseat full of food, he got behind the wheel and waited for Bree to come out with another bag of ice. Celia was following them in her car, and foot by foot, mile by mile, they made it down the canyon and into town.

Beau's house had a long driveway that he'd obviously been out to shovel already that day. Andrew pulled up as far as he could, because at least three other cars would need to fit. Celia parked beside him, and the three of them got all the food inside.

It was warm in Beau's house, and Andrew gave his younger brother a big hug. "Thanks for hosting," he said. "This place looks great."

"That's because of Deirdre." Beau nodded to someone behind Andrew, and Andrew turned to see a gloriously radiant woman standing there. She was nervous as a cat in a room full of rocking chairs, if the way her lip trembled and how she wound her hands around themselves indicated anything.

"My brother, Andrew," Beau said, approaching her with caution. Andrew had no idea what was going on. His mom had said something about a case, but this didn't seem like that. This was...babysitting.

"Andrew, this is Deirdre. She's a client of mine that needed somewhere to be for a little while." Beau, ever the lawyer, spoke in riddles and vague undertones Andrew used to want to figure out. Today, though, he simply shook Deirdre's hand and introduced Celia and Bree.

"Put us to work, Celia," he said, and she did. Beau and Deirdre set the table, and Andrew noticed them with their heads bent together, talking, more than once.

He put the yams and stuffing in the oven to warm again, and Bree started slicing the celery and cucumbers they'd brought from the lodge. Celia made gravy from the drippings of the turkey that Beau had roasted that morning, and then she put together a ranch dip to go with the veggie tray Bree had finished.

With only minutes until lunchtime, Graham and his family arrived, followed by their mother and Eli, Meg, and Stockton.

The atmosphere was vibrant and celebratory. Andrew gripped Eli's shoulders tight and said, "How's California?" He hadn't thought he'd missed his younger brother quite so much, but he had.

"California's great. I thought you were going to come." Eli stepped back and looked at Andrew, dozens of questions and implications in his eyes.

"I was. I am. Maybe in January when we've got ten feet of snow on the ground."

Meg laughed, and Andrew gave her a hug too. "You guys should come see the horses while you're here." They'd just gotten in last night, Andrew knew that. They'd driven to their mother's where they were staying.

"Yeah!" Stockton cheered. "Do you still have the snowshoes at the lodge, Uncle Andrew?"

"We sure do, bud." He glanced out the window. "And there will probably be enough snow by tomorrow to go."

"Can we, Dad?" Stockton turned to Eli, who smiled down at his son.

"We'll see, Stocky. We have plans with Grandma for something."

"Movie," Meg said softly. "Double date." She put her finger to her lips like the date was a secret and glanced over her shoulder to where Andrew's mother worked in the kitchen with Celia.

"Who's she going out with this time?" Andrew asked.

"You're still upset about it?" Eli asked.

"I'm not upset." He just didn't understand. "Who is it?"

"Dave Dirkle."

Andrew rolled his eyes and moved away to ask Bailey if she wanted to come snowshoeing tomorrow too.

"Sure," Laney said. "Stockton will be with us all afternoon, and he loves snowshoeing."

At least Andrew wasn't the only Whittaker who didn't always know what was going on. He wondered if he got married, if Becca would keep track of things like who his mother was dating and when they were babysitting a niece or nephew.

Like lightning had struck him, he realized he'd just pictured himself married to Becca. His heart wailed, but Celia said, "Time to eat," and everyone gathered over by the bar to say grace.

Andrew felt incomplete during the meal, even when he expressed his gratitude for his family, the food, and the great year they'd had at Springside. Everyone else at the table had someone, and he didn't.

Even if Beau's guest was a client, and his mother's was an old friend they now employed. He still felt all alone amidst the people he loved most, and that was because there was someone who he loved who wasn't there.

After dinner, while his mom started a pot of coffee and the pies were set on the counter to come to room temperature, he sat down beside Graham and said, "I need to get Becca back. Tell me what to do."

Eli immediately put his phone down and leaned forward. "Becca?"

"I need to get her back." Andrew flicked a glance in Eli's direction. "You guys managed to get women to marry you. Help me." He obviously wasn't above begging, and Graham gave him a big smile.

"Okay, here's what you do...."

CHAPTER 20

B ecca spent an hour each day before work looking for a new job. She thought she wanted to work at the mayor's office, maybe get more involved in the political side of things, as she enjoyed public policy and fighting for what she believed in.

But she was wrong. This job was boring, didn't fulfill her, and she wanted to leave two minutes after she arrived.

But a few weeks before Christmas didn't seem to be a great time to find a job, as there didn't seem to be much going on locally besides food service.

At this point, she was almost willing to don an apron and take orders, because the thought of sitting at her desk for another day was almost enough to drive her insane. She'd avoided going to church, because she knew Andrew went. She'd been praying for a solution to her problem, but there seemed to be a lot of doors open, and she wasn't even sure which one she should approach.

By the Wednesday after Thanksgiving, she couldn't take it anymore. With no answers from on high, she knocked lightly on the mayor's door, knowing he was inside the office as she'd seen him arrive an hour ago.

"Mayor Berry?" she asked, pushing the door open a few inches.

He glanced up, and said, "Becca? Come on in." He sounded pleasant, but he didn't add a smile to his statement. In the past, before Andrew had forgotten to inform the mayor about the SonarBot, he would've smiled. Maybe jumped from his desk to shake her hand.

Now, he leaned onto his arms as she approached. She sat down and smoothed her palms down her thighs. "This isn't a good fit for me," she said. "I'm looking for another job, and I wanted to give notice here in case you need to replace me." Why he was paying her to read articles and make lists, she wasn't sure. It wasn't an election year, and she really did nothing for him.

He slid his glasses from his nose. "That's fine. When would you like to be done?"

"How much longer do you need me?"

"Honestly, Becca, I don't need you. I offered you the job, because I think you're a great public speaker and press secretary, and if you wanted to be on my team, I wanted you."

Becca's pride swelled with the compliment. "Thank you, sir. I think maybe today would be a good day to be done."

He stood, nodded, and shook her hand. She left his office lighter than she'd felt for a month. Pausing at her desk, she looked around for any personal items. She had her coffee mug and a picture of Otto…and not much else.

Since she didn't really have anything to do, she started cruising the job boards, deciding on the spot to apply for a wait-ressing position. She could deliver bacon and eggs, make small talk, and probably do well in tips.

She walked out of the mayor's office by noon, with an interview at the steakhouse that afternoon. Maybe it wasn't what someone with two college degrees should be doing. But it was better than doing nothing, and better than going back to Andrew and begging for her job back.

She'd thought for a few moments a few weeks ago, that she and Andrew might have another shot at a relationship. She'd listened to his message and heard him say he missed her and wondered if they could get together when he got back to Coral Canyon.

But then he'd never called. She'd gone to Crystal Lake for the Thanksgiving holidays, and while her mom had asked her if she was seeing anyone, Becca hadn't told them about Andrew.

Because she and Andrew weren't together. She wasn't seeing him, not anymore. And the thought of going through the Christmas season alone was enough to make her want to hibernate until the snow melted.

She was hired on the spot for a waitressing position at Lonestar's Steakhouse, and she started that evening as a shadow to another waiter.

John taught her how to put in orders, make the frozen lemonades, and bounce from table to table. She refilled drinks and took checks, learned how to process cards, and forgot to eat she was so busy. And it was a Wednesday night.

She couldn't imagine what a weekend would be like. "Insane," John said as they wiped down the tables, refilled salt shakers, and arranged the condiments on the table. "But great tips."

The next day, she went into the steakhouse in the morning and shadowed another waitress on the lunch crowd. Apparently that was a harder shift to staff for her manager, Lisa, and Becca said she'd be glad to fill it.

By Friday, she was on her own, waiting on the lunch crowd solo and loving it. Sure, she made a few mistakes, but they weren't so important she couldn't recover. She liked the busyness of it, while the job remained low stress. After all, if she said the wrong thing, there were no cameras recording it.

When she returned home at night, she was tired, something that hadn't happened since the tour. She laid her head back against the couch and sighed as Otto jumped up beside her.

"Hey, bud. What did you do today?" She scrubbed along his jaw and neck. "Let me guess. You took a nap." She grinned at the dog, who seemed to smile back.

She pushed herself back off the couch, her aching feet protesting. But the Friday lunch crowd had been thick and they left great tips. "We've got to check the bowls in the back." She didn't let Otto out with her, because he tended to go right for the muddy spots against the fence.

Instead, she stepped into her big snow boots and gathered all the bowls at once. No wasted time outside in the frigid Wyoming winter. She washed out the ice and debris inside, filled some with food and some with water and dashed back outside to deliver the bowls to whichever animals needed them.

Her stomach grumbled, but she didn't have the energy to make herself something to eat. "Should we get pizza or Chinese?" she asked her dog. It hadn't snowed that day, so the delivery drivers would still be out, and she opened the drawer beside her microwave to check her take-out menus.

"Chinese," she said, because pizza reminded her too much of Andrew.

She picked up the phone to place her order, but she couldn't decide between the beef and broccoli and the tiny spicy chicken.

"Can't get tiny spicy," she muttered to herself, as that was when she and Andrew had enjoyed their first kiss. Maybe she should call Andrew and he could bring her the Chinese food. Before she could decide what to do, a knock sounded on her front door.

Otto barked once, and she shushed him. She approached the door slowly as the wind whistled around the corners of her house. Whoever was out there had to be slightly insane or in serious trouble.

She opened the door partway, expecting to see a neighbor.

"Andrew." The outside air stuck in her lungs, and he looked positively frozen.

He lifted a plastic sack with a few containers in it. "I brought Chinese food."

She had no idea what to say. How had he known she was about to order Chinese?

"I can't keep living like this," he said. "I miss you." He swallowed. "I'm sorry about what I said in...wherever we were. It was all a lie, just to get Dwight's focus off of us. You have never annoyed me, and I'm in love with you."

He shifted his weight, his eyes hopeful but worried too. "That's it," he said. "That's all I have prepared to say."

Becca's face stretched into a smile, and her eyes felt so hot. She realized she was crying when the first tear splashed on her cheek. "Come in," she said in a high-pitched voice. "It's freezing out here."

She stepped back and he came in. With the door closed behind him, he filled the space with the scent of his cologne and tiny spicy chicken. He went all the way into the kitchen and turned around to face her, tucking his hands in his pockets and stalling at the edge of the living room.

"So you work at the steakhouse now," he finally said.

That same spark and electricity that had always been between them arced across the room. Becca took a step forward, having imagined him here in her house but unsure what to do now that it was a reality.

"You really didn't mean any of those things?" She disliked that she seemed to be leaking from every hole in her face.

"Becca," he spoke with complete tenderness in his voice. In that moment, she realized he was wearing his cowboy jeans. Those boots. And a denim jacket that made him more country than business. All he was missing was the hat, but he'd still come to her as his authentic self.

"I'm so miserable without you," he said. "I'm so, so sorry for what I said. None of it was true. Please." His voice broke, and he looked away while he composed himself. "I didn't mean any of it."

"I'd told you how men weren't attracted to me for long." She wiped her tears. "That really hurt."

"I know." He took another step toward her. "I suppose I'm not like most men, because I'm hopelessly attracted to you." Another step. "Just tell me what to do, and I'll do it."

Becca wasn't sure what to tell him. He'd showed up with food. He'd apologized. And he kept saying all the right things.

I'm in love with you.

He'd said hard, heart-felt things. Becca said, "I love you too."

Andrew's face burst into a smile and he hurried to close the space between them. He cradled her face, his eyes so bright and so beautiful. "I'm sorry."

"You've said it a bunch of times." She traced one fingertip along his eyebrow. "I believe you."

He kissed her then, and Becca felt all the wounds in her soul heal with that simple touch of his lips to hers.

An hour later, she'd eaten, told him about the catastrophe that was the job at the mayor's office, and confessed that yes, she did work at the steakhouse now. He sat on the couch, and she leaned against him, the feel of his arms around her and his solid chest behind her one of the most comforting things to her.

He hadn't offered her the job at Springside, and she honestly wasn't sure she'd even take it if he did. She rather liked being his girlfriend and not his co-worker. Well, she'd liked it all, but if she had to pick one, she'd take girlfriend.

"So I haven't seen you at church," he said, rubbing slow circles on her arm with his thumb.

"I was afraid of running into you."

"I'm wondering if you'd go with me this weekend. I'm so tired of sitting by myself."

Becca understood the feeling. "I'd like that," she whispered. Peace flowed through her, and she knew Andrew was the right man for her. So he'd made a mistake. He'd apologized—finally. And he loved her. She'd felt the truth in those words as soon as he'd said them.

"I'd also like to invite you to come to the lodge for Christmas." He tensed for a moment. "I'm not sure if you have plans with your family or not."

"Not yet." She ran her fingers along his knuckles, eventually clasping both of her hands around his one.

"My family does a big tree lighting on Christmas Eve," he said. "It's been a tradition since my dad died, and I'm wondering if you'd like to help me pick a tree, decorate it, and come to our friends and family dinner that night."

"It sounds too good to be true."

He chuckled. "Well, it's not that. But we do have stockings for everyone, and everyone gets a little gift or two. The food is great. And someone special gets to light the tree."

"Who's doing it this year?" she asked.

"I am."

"You think you're something special, don't you?"

He pressed his lips to her temple. "Not without you. I am not complete without you."

They were perfect words, from the perfect man. Becca couldn't help smiling, and she twisted as she said, "I'd love to come to your family tree lighting and dinner."

"Great." He kissed her again, and the love Becca had for him spiraled through her.

CHAPTER 21

Andrew shivered in the saddle, the chill of the wind snaking down his collar as Wolfgang clip-clopped through the snow toward the copse of pine trees on the hill.

Becca rode a few steps behind him, and he called, "You okay?"

"It's *freezing* out here," she said, and he chuckled.

"Yes, it is." He'd already been out to this stand of trees and selected a large tree for the foyer at the lodge. "But this should be quick."

The swooshing of the sleigh runners behind him soothed him, but not as much as having Becca with him. "See the one with the orange flag?" He pointed just up ahead. "It's that one."

"And you're going to cut that thing down?" Becca sounded like such a feat was impossible. "It's huge."

"The foyer is huge." Andrew was undeterred. He brought Wolfgang to a halt and swung off the horse's back to collect the chainsaw from the sleigh. "And I'm not going to hack it down with an axe." He positioned his sound-canceling earphones over his ears. "Put in your earplugs."

When she was ready, she gave him a thumbs-up, and he pulled

the ripcord on the chainsaw, and an earsplitting roar filled the air. He'd read a half-dozen articles on how to make a tree fall the way he wanted it to, and watched two videos. He made the notch on the side of the tree where it should fall—away from himself, Becca, and the horses—and rounded the tree to start cutting.

Sixty seconds later, the tree trunk cracked and the tree fell exactly where he wanted it to. He waited for the chainsaw to stop vibrating in his hands. "Now's the hard part." Getting the tree onto the sleigh. That, and getting it into the house, but Graham said he'd come help with that.

Andrew tied the chainsaw back into place on the sleigh, and started uncoiling the rope he'd brought. "I'm going to loop it around one of the branches," he said as he tromped through the snow. "And then use the stump like a pulley." They weren't the only ones who'd been up to this section of the mountain. It had been reserved for those who liked to go choose and chop their own tree, and as Andrew heaved, the sound of a motor met his ears.

Wolfgang shifted his feet, and Andrew darted over to grab the reins and hand them to Becca. He scanned the horizon to find a couple of ATVs headed their way. He went back to pulling, getting the tree closer and closer to the sleigh.

"Need a hand?" Two men climbed off their four-wheelers and came over to help him heave the tree onto the sleigh. With three of them, they had the tree tied down and ready in only a few minutes.

"Thanks." Andrew grinned at them and shook their hands. "Do you two need help?"

"Nah, we're taking one about a third that size." They smiled back and returned to their ATVs.

"A third," Becca said, giving him a *told-you* look as he took Wolfgang's reins.

"Have you seen the lodge?" Andrew said. "I'm not putting some piddly tree in there on my year." He shook his head.

"Nope. Not gonna happen. The tree lighting is a big thing for us Whittakers."

Becca wasn't technically a Whittaker, and Andrew almost blurted that he'd bought her a diamond for Christmas. He barely caught the words on his tongue before they were spoken, and he swallowed until he felt like he wouldn't spill his secret.

There was a gift exchange on Christmas Eve—only another week away—and she'd get the ring then. His stomach writhed just thinking about it. They'd talked a bit about marriage, but not much, and she'd never really given him a straightforward answer anyway.

But he didn't want to live in that giant lodge by himself anymore. She had a perfectly good house in town, and he liked her dog, and the commute to Springside would be much less.

Graham met him on the porch, and said, "All right. Let's get this beast inside." He took in the length of the downed tree. "Andrew, it's going to be great." He clapped his hand on Andrew's shoulder. "It's a beautiful tree."

Andrew's chest filled with warmth though he was sure he was only moments away from frostbite. And when Becca slipped her hand into his, he just knew this was going to be the best Christmas ever.

———

A FEW DAYS LATER, HE WOKE WHEN OTTO STARTED LICKING HIS fingers. He jerked away from the slobbery tongue and took a moment to realize he'd fallen asleep on Becca's couch, Becca curled into him.

"Hey," she said. "I knew you'd fall asleep."

"You sound like you did too."

"Maybe." She grinned, and Andrew let the soft, lazy moment between them linger.

"I should go," he said, wondering what time it was. It would be frigid outside, and the thought already had his muscles tight.

"I wish you never had to go." She snuggled deeper into his chest so he couldn't see her face.

"Yeah? Does that mean you want to talk about getting married?"

She tensed in his arms for a quick moment, a breath, and then she relaxed. "Yeah, I think we should probably get married."

Andrew leaned back though he didn't have much room. He gained enough to be able to look into her eyes. "Yeah?"

A small smile tugged at the corners of her mouth. "Yeah. I love you, and I don't want you to go up to that lodge at night anymore."

"I don't either." He kissed her, letting the love he felt for her stream through him. "I love you, Becca."

Happiness romped through him, and he thought this might be the closest to joy he'd ever experienced. "Do you see yourself as a winter bride? Or are we waiting for spring? Summer?"

"I can get a shawl or a cape," she said. "Because I want to marry you as soon as possible."

"All right then."

"We better go ring shopping," she said. "I bet they're having some good sales right now."

Andrew blinked, and she said, "What?"

"Um, I may have already bought you a ring."

That got her to pull away from him a bit more. "You did?"

"Maybe." He shrugged, though he wasn't trying to be convincing at all.

"When were you going to tell me?"

"It's in your stocking at the lodge."

"Right now?"

"Yes."

Her eyes searched his, and he couldn't tell if he'd made a mistake or not. "I was hoping you'd be ready by then. Turns out, I was right."

Becca gave him a playful push against his chest and started

laughing. "I'm so glad you told me," she said. "I can't imagine pulling that out in front of your family."

"My family loves you. Why would that be a problem?"

"It's just...feels like this is an intimate moment. Something private between me and you."

"So you'd like me to get that out of your stocking before tomorrow night."

"Yes, please."

"Well, I'll see what I can do. Celia watches those stockings like a hawk."

"Sure, okay," she said as she rolled her eyes. "I'm sure you'll figure something out."

———

The following day, Becca arrived at the lodge by mid-afternoon, having finished her lunchtime shift at the steakhouse. They put the finishing touches on the tree and moved into the kitchen to help Celia with any dinner preparations.

But she shooed them away, and they ended up at the bar with hot chocolate and a plate of crispy rice treats that had caramel and peanut butter in them.

Andrew ate too much sugar and felt a bit jittery as a result. Or maybe that was because he'd gotten the ring out of Becca's stocking an hour before she'd arrived and now carried it in his pocket.

"You want to go riding?" he asked. "I think we have an hour or so before people will start arriving."

Becca did not want to go riding—Andrew could tell just by looking at her. So much was said as they looked at one another, and she ended up saying, "Sure. Let me get my coat."

Andrew shrugged into his coat too, and Becca joined him in the mudroom so they could go out the back door and down the sidewalk toward the stables. He stuck his hands in his pockets, and felt the cold metal of the ring in his right one.

"So do you want to see the ring?" he asked.

She stalled and looked at him. "You have it with you?"

He withdrew it and kept it hidden in his palm. "It's nothing special. Just sort of a placeholder ring, and then we can go pick one you like." He wasn't sure why he felt like someone had poured wasps into his bloodstream.

He hadn't planned a big proposal; hadn't even thought about it. But faced with her, and holding the ring, he couldn't just shove it on her finger and say, "Done."

So he dropped to both knees and held the ring up toward her. "I love you, Becca. I'd love to see you in a snow-white cape when you become my wife. Will you marry me?"

Becca held very still, her eyes locked on his. Then she switched her gaze to the ring and took it from him. "This is beautiful." She started to slide it on her own finger, and Andrew jumped to his feet.

"Wait, wait." He gently took the ring from her, kept his eyes on it, and said, "You haven't even said yes yet."

"Do I really need to say yes?"

He lifted his eyes to hers. "Yes."

She grinned, clearly teasing him, and threw her arms around him. "Yes, Andrew. A million times yes." She kissed him, and giggled like a schoolgirl as he slid the tiny diamond band on her left ring finger.

"I love you," he murmured before kissing her again.

By the time they made it back to the house, everyone had arrived. The foyer was full of chatter and laughter, with people going around and putting small, wrapped gifts in each stocking. Andrew stood with his hand in Becca's, basking in the glow of the holiday spirit.

"There he is." His mom spotted him and came over. "Celia said you went riding."

"Yeah," Andrew said, though they hadn't even gone into the stables. His nose and ears tingled as they warmed, and he edged a bit closer to the roaring fire in the hearth.

Beau went around to the stockings and said, "Okay, I think we're ready."

Graham was already sitting on the couch, his son on his lap. Bailey and Laney sat next to them, and Laney stopped talking to Meg. Stockton sat on the floor, and Eli loitered near the front door, never one to just sit down and relax.

Beau took a spot on the loveseat next to Deirdre, who looked as nervous now as she had at Thanksgiving. She seemed like she'd gained a bit of weight though, and Andrew realized in that moment that everyone was looking at him.

"Welcome to the lodge," he said, his voice maybe a bit too loud. "It's good to have everyone here." Of course, everyone was not there, and he took an extra long couple of moments to remember his father and the last Christmas they'd had with him.

"First, we'll light the tree, like we always do. Becca and I selected it, chopped it down, and decorated it." His voice tightened, as it seemed like they'd already started traditions of their own.

He cleared his throat. "Then we'll do the stockings. You just take yours and open the little gifts inside. Then Celia has dinner in the dining room. I think Bree made the name plates this year, and they're actually Christmas ornaments." He met her eye. "Right?"

She nodded, smiling around at the family.

"All right then. I'll light the tree." Andrew took a breath, but before he could move to go light the tree, his mother said, "Really? You're not going to make any other announcements?"

Andrew looked at her, aware of Becca's movement to his left. A squeal rose up from the women in the room, and Andrew swung his attention to Becca.

She was holding her left hand up, palm back so everyone could see the diamond ring. Andrew got jostled as his mother, Laney, and Meg all swarmed. His mother grabbed onto Andrew and said, "Congratulations, Andy."

She was the only person on earth who ever called him that, and it made his emotion surge and stick in the back of his throat.

After he'd hugged his brothers and the excitement over the ring—which totally wasn't warranted, in Andrew's opinion—he said, "So can I light the tree now?"

"Hey, you upstaged yourself," Graham said, chuckling.

"At least I don't drive a minivan," Andrew shot back.

Graham rolled his eyes while Laney laughed, and Andrew stepped over to the light switch that would illuminate the tree. "All right," he said. "Three, two, one…."

He pressed the switch, and the tree burst to life, with bright, all-white lights that reflected off the silver and gold ornaments.

"Look at the little reindeer nose," Stockton said, and Meg led him over to the tree to see the other decorations close up.

Andrew took Becca's hand in his and gazed at the tree.

"It's spectacular," she whispered. "Thank you for inviting me."

"Becca, I dreamed of having you here." The glow from the Christmas lights made her seem even more angelic, and Andrew gazed at his fiancée with so much love coursing through him.

"Merry Christmas," he whispered just before kissing her.

———

Read on for a sneak peek at **HER COWBOY BILLIONAIRE BODYGUARD**, featuring Andrew's brother, Beau, and the woman who comes to him for help to protect her music career. **Now available in paperback!**

SNEAK PEEK! HER COWBOY BILLIONAIRE BODYGUARD CHAPTER ONE

B eau Whittaker resisted the urge to reach up and brush the tiny hairs from the back of his neck. Celia always swatted his hand away when he did, and she'd clean him up anyway. But they sure did itch.

He supposed he should be used to all the itching when it came to hair, as he'd grown a full beard over the course of the last ten months, and he only let Celia shave the back and sides of his head to maintain some sort of respect when he went down the canyon to church. Or maybe he did it for his mother, so she wouldn't reprimand him for letting himself totally turn into a recluse. Or had she said hermit?

It didn't matter. Beau was tired of defending himself. With Andrew out of the lodge now, and living with his new wife in town, someone needed to live at Whiskey Mountain Lodge and take care of the horses. So what if Beau had let his hair grow out in the process? Didn't mean he'd cut himself off from society.

Even if he had.

Celia hummed as she kept the clippers running along his scalp. Across the counter, a pot of soup bubbled, putting off the scent of chicken broth and cooked carrots and freshly made pasta. The only thing that could cover the mouth-watering smell of Celia's town-famous chicken noodle soup was the bread she served with it.

The bowl holding the proofing dough sat beside the stove, and Beau couldn't wait until his haircut was finished. Then he could get these itchy hairs off his neck, and Celia would start kneading and forming rolls. Once he showered and slicked some gel through his hair, the scent of freshly baked bread would fill this kitchen.

And then, only a bit after that, *L. Rhett* would arrive. Beau's muscles bunched at the thought. He knew whoever had been emailing him these past few weeks had been using a pseudonym, as well as a brand new email account. He wasn't even sure if he was meeting a man or a woman, which was why he'd asked his oldest brother, Graham, to come to the lodge a few minutes before this Rhett person was set to arrive.

Beau hoped the case would be worthwhile, as he hadn't done much but grow hair and ride horses for a few months now. At the same time, those two things had been exactly what he'd needed in his life, to soothe his ego and to calm his ragged soul. Somehow, sitting in church every week hadn't done that, as there were so many female eyes watching him. Filled with sympathy at what had happened with his last case—and the woman at the center of it he'd let into his heart.

He exhaled, wishing he could find all the pieces of his most vital organ, and held completely still while Celia finished his haircut.

"There you go," she finally said, whipping the brush across his neck and ears. She unpinned the drape from around his neck, and he stood to face her.

"Thank you, Celia."

"Do you want to eat now or after you shower?"

"After." He clenched his fist so he wouldn't reach up to touch his neck. "And Graham's coming over."

"Don't I know it? He's texted me five times about sending

soup home for his family." Celia gave a light laugh and shook her head. "It's a miracle they all haven't starved."

Beau chuckled too and headed down the hall and into the master bedroom. Every one of his brothers had lived in this room at some point over the last few years, but Beau had added the most to the room.

He'd put up pictures of their family, asked Annie to get him some real paintings of the area from local artists, and in the middle of it all, he'd placed a picture of his mom and dad on the day they got married.

He glanced at the photograph now, a twinge of missing racing through him at the familiar face he found on his dad. It was the same one he saw every time he looked into a mirror. Well, before the beard, at least.

Beau paused to look at his mother. Only eighteen when she married his dad, Beau's mother was the strongest person he knew. She'd raised four boys almost alone as her husband built the largest energy company in Wyoming and ran it for fourteen hours a day, seven days a week.

He was the only brother who'd never left Coral Canyon, except for a few years to finish law school, and he was the only one who was here the day his dad died.

He ran his fingers along the top of the metal picture frame and sighed, wondering if this meeting was a good idea or not. Beau thought himself a good judge of character, even when the only communication he'd had was through email. And whoever had been conversing with him was in a desperate state.

"Desperate people do desperate things," he muttered to himself as he went to shower. When he returned to the kitchen, complete with his cowboy hat and boots, Graham sat at the counter along with a bowl of soup and three buttered rolls.

"You're early," Beau said, settling onto a barstool beside his brother.

"Mm," Graham said, his mouth full of food and rendering him unable to talk.

But when Celia put a steaming bowl of soup and a plate of rolls in front of Beau, he decided talking was quite overrated too. Especially when there was eating to be done.

Graham finished before him, and asked, "So who's coming over?"

Beau kept chewing as he tried to figure out how to answer his brother. After swallowing, he said, "Hopefully a new client."

"And you need me here for that?"

"She's obviously not telling me who she really is."

"Then how do you know it's a woman?" The wind rattled the windows behind them in the dining room.

"I don't. I just have a feeling," Beau said. "She wouldn't show me her case, but insisted that we meet to go over things." He glanced at the blue numbers on the microwave. "She should be here soon."

Graham shook his head and reached for his fourth roll. "If you think it's a woman, what am I doing here?"

"Getting dinner for your family." Beau elbowed him slightly and dunked a piece of his bread in his soup. "And taking Daisy for a couple of days, remember?"

"Oh, right." He glanced around for Beau's Rottweiler. She perked up from her dog bed in the corner of the kitchen. "I guess Bailey needs to draw her for art." He sounded less than thrilled to have a second dog, even for a few days. "I'm not sure why Bear isn't good enough."

"Too old," Beau joked. "How are Laney and the kids?"

"Just fine," Graham said. Beau saw them all the time anyway, especially now that he lived out at the lodge.

Jealousy touched Beau for just a moment. There, then gone. He wanted a house full of kids, like the one he'd grown up in. His mother kept telling him he had plenty of time, but he was almost twice her age when she'd gotten married, and he couldn't even entice a scared woman who'd he'd helped to stay in town and give their relationship a chance.

Oh, no. Deirdre had chosen her old life down in Colorado over Beau.

His chest pinched and he took an enormous bite of his roll, hoping to quell it. He finished eating, and he and Graham put their dishes in the dishwasher. He'd just stepped into the living room and switched on the fireplace when knocking sounded on the front door.

Graham, who'd just sank into the couch, stood again and met Beau's eyes. "I guess that's her."

Beau ran his hands over his beard and straightened his shoulders. He'd met hundreds of clients over the years, but for some reason this one felt different. He didn't get a lot of anonymity in Coral Canyon, as everyone knew everyone else's business. But this person wasn't from Coral Canyon, he knew that much.

After all, Graham was a tech genius, and he'd tracked the email address to an IP server out of Jackson Hole. Only an hour away, Jackson was at least four times as big as Coral Canyon, with plenty of tourists to gossip about.

He strode over to the door and opened it, Graham right beside him. Together, they stood shoulder to shoulder, filling the doorway and creating a very physical barrier to whoever stood on the stoop.

Sure enough, a woman stood there, haloed in the porch light.

Beau stared as he drank in her long, almost white hair, slight frame, and fair features. She sucked in a breath, her blue eyes turning cold at the same time she deftly reached into her purse and pulled out a canister. She expertly positioned her finger on the top and said, "Who are you?"

Beau couldn't speak, and he wasn't even sure why. His muscles had cinched at the sight of the pepper spray, but really it was this woman's beauty that had rendered him mute and still.

"You rang our doorbell," Graham said easily, leaning his shoulder into the doorframe on his side. Beau still couldn't so much as move, or even blink.

"Which one of you is Beau Whittaker?"

Graham hooked his thumb at Beau. "That'd be him."

Beau lifted his arm, but he didn't have any conscious thought about it. Why couldn't he get his voice to work? He'd never been tongue-tied in all of his thirty-four years, but this woman had stolen his very words from him.

The woman glanced over her shoulder and apparently decided that nothing was going to jump out and attack her, as her finger slipped off the nozzle of the canister.

Graham elbowed Beau in the ribs, which made him go, "Oof," and curl into himself protectively. He glared at his brother, and Graham lifted his eyebrows and chin-nodded toward the beautiful woman still standing on their doorstep.

Beau's face heated, and he managed to take a step backward. "I'm Beau Whittaker," he said, extending his hand for the woman to shake. His skin tingled in anticipation of touching her, and he promptly commanded himself to calm down. "You must be L. Rhett?"

Her eyes flew to his, and he realized in that moment that she'd forgotten the fake name she'd used in her correspondence with him.

Didn't matter. Beau would be getting this woman's real name and phone number, and his prayers that he'd get this new case shifted to an entirely different level, for an entirely different reason.

SNEAK PEEK! HER COWBOY BILLIONAIRE BODYGUARD CHAPTER TWO

L ily Everett had taken her finger off the nozzle of her pepper spray, but she hadn't committed to putting it fully away. Unsure as to why, she reached out with her other hand and shook Beau's.

He was a big bear of a man, just like his email had said. If bears wore big, black cowboy hats, that was. Which he did, and he looked pretty amazing doing it.

Problem was, the other man standing next to him also wore a cowboy hat and stood easily as wide, equally as bear-like. She pumped Beau's hand a couple of times, glad her father had taught her how to give a proper handshake before flying across the ocean to the Middle East, where he conducted business with his oil company.

"This is my brother, Graham," Beau said. "He just came up for a quick bite to eat." Beau turned to Graham. "I'm sure Celia has your food ready to take down to your family."

Lily didn't miss the hidden message beneath Beau's words, and she released his hand and looked at his brother simultaneously.

"Nice to meet you," Graham said as if he hadn't gotten the hint that Beau wanted him to leave. "And you are…?"

Both brothers stood there, watching her, but Lily really didn't want to give her name. *They've already stared you down,* she thought, and they hadn't exclaimed or sucked in their breath as they recognized her. Nothing.

"Lily Everett," she finally said, shifting her feet back as if expecting to be hit with their realizations.

"Well, c'mon in," Beau said, stepping back. "We're not going to talk on the porch."

Lily had no sooner stepped into the huge lodge before a woman appeared in the doorway. "I'm headed out, boys. Graham, your food is on the counter." Her eyes landed on Lily, and she smiled for two moments before recognition lit her eyes. "Oh, hello. Sorry, I didn't see you there."

Lily's heart thumped in her chest, sounding like a bass drum in her ears, while she waited for the woman to exclaim over who she was, and which song was her favorite. Then the questions came—*how do you come up with the lyrics for the songs? Are your sisters as beautiful as you? Who taught you to play the piano?*

But the woman just smiled and said, "I'm Celia, but I'm also leaving," as she slipped past the two brothers and past Lily before pulling the front door closed behind her.

"You can put that pepper spray away," Beau said. "I'm not going to bite, and my brother is leaving."

"Oh, right." Graham sprang toward the doorway Celia had come through, leaving Lily alone with Beau. She'd met thousands of people in her life, and she couldn't sense a single ounce of danger surrounding him. So he was a great big *teddy* bear of a man, and Lily couldn't help the way her heart started thumping again.

This time, it wasn't over fear of being discovered for who she was. It was because he stirred something in her that had been dormant for many years. Something Lily had never expected to be so much as disturbed again.

And it's not now, she told herself. *Don't be ridiculous.* She needed Beau's help to get Kent off her back once and for all. She was not interested in the man for much more than his legal skills —and he was the best in the surrounding five states, if her research was correct.

"Would you like to sit?" He chose a chair near the fireplace, which flickered with false flames.

She perched on the edge of the couch across from him, a large, square coffee table between them. Slipping the pepper spray back into her purse, she crossed her legs and peered at Beau. "Thank you for meeting with me."

"Oh, the only things keepin' me busy around here are a few horses." He smiled at her, a warm, made-of-honey smile that helped her relax another notch. He looked like the type of man who could break a horse in a single afternoon.

He startled just a bit, a little flinch, and cleared his throat. "Did you bring your case files?" Beau glanced to her purse, which certainly wasn't large enough for the files he needed. All at once, Lily remembered why she was there and it wasn't to meet a man or get a date.

It was to get her dirty, no-good, cheating ex-husband out of her life for good.

"I just wanted to meet," she said, finding her voice. "If I decide to hire you, then you'll have full access to my files."

"All right," he said easily as if he had conversations like this every evening. Maybe he did, but Lily certainly didn't, and though this was probably one of the most expensive couches she'd ever sat on, she shifted and couldn't find a comfortable spot.

Clearly this Beau Whittaker had some money of his own. The thought actually appealed to Lily quite a lot, as she'd had her fair share of "suitors" who were only interested in her to get closer to her bank account.

Like Kent.

"So what do you need to know, Miss Lily?" Beau relaxed further into his chair, almost like he was fixing to take a nap.

With the way the house smelled like warm bread and chicken broth, Lily could see why.

"I'm wondering if you can tell me a little bit about yourself," she said, putting a wall between her and everything else. She'd perfected such things over the years, as she needed to appear to love her fans but also keep them at arm's distance. She had to seem like she adored being on stage even when her heart was broken, or she had a terrible head cold, or she hadn't slept in days.

Oh, yes, Lily Everett could perform and pretend better than almost anyone. And she could ignore these twittering feelings in her stomach and focus on the real reason she'd come all the way to Coral Canyon and then up another canyon to meet this man. This lawyer. And weren't all lawyers sharks? Kent certainly had been.

"Let's see," Beau said. "I'm the youngest of four brothers. Graham, he's the oldest." His voice settled into an easy rhythm with a definite country twang, which matched the cowboy hat effortlessly.

"I used to have a law office in town, but the work got…monotonous."

Lily sensed something else behind that word, but she simply nodded so he'd go on. "So I switched things up a little. My brothers have all lived in this lodge and it was empty, so I moved up here. Closed my office and started taking on select clients."

"What kind of clients?" She'd heard through the underground about what he did. But she wanted to hear him say it.

"Women in trouble," he said unapologetically and with compassion and determination in those dark, dreamy eyes.

Lyrics sprang to her head, something she normally embraced. Slowed down her life so she could take notes.

With eyes as dark as his
A woman has no choice
But to fall.

Lily shook herself. She would not *fall* into another pair of brown eyes, no matter how chocolatey and delicious they seemed. She pushed the lyrics away, determined not to write a song inspired by this man in front of her.

"Women who need somewhere safe to stay while we work on their case," he continued. "The lodge provides an...out-of-the-way place for protection, and I still have all the resources I need here."

"Do you ever go to court? Or do you usually settle?"

Beau leaned forward, a flame in his expression now that matched the fireplace he sat beside. "I aim to settle," he said. "And I usually do, according to my terms, in about ninety-nine percent of the cases I take."

"How long have you been doing this?" she asked.

"You'd be my fifth client," he said. "Under this type of arrangement."

"What credentials do you have to be a bodyguard?"

He blinked and leaned back into his chair, most of his face getting swallowed by the shadows cast from the brim of his hat. "I've never claimed to be a bodyguard."

"Well, that's what they call you out there."

Cocking his head, he asked, "Out where?"

She gestured in the general direction of the front door. "Out where I heard about you."

Beau let several beats of silence flow between them. Lily couldn't be sure, but he seemed to be sizing her up far too easily. Or maybe he was working through some zinging, troubling feelings of his own.

"Let's be clear," he said slowly, the rumbly quality of his voice soothing and terrifying at the same time. "If I take you on as a client, yes, you'd live here in the lodge with me. The remote location offers protection, and I suppose I manage to do so as well. We'll work on your case and get you the relief you need."

Relief. Lily wanted relief so badly, she almost sagged into the soft couch behind her.

"What's the fee?" she asked, keeping her back straight, straight, straight.

"To live here? Or to hire me?"

"Both," she said. He obviously didn't recognize her, and she didn't need him to know she could probably buy this lodge and employ him.

"The room and board is free," he said. "You have to treat Celia, Annie, and Bree kindly, and it wouldn't kill you to help out around the house or with the horses. But it's not required."

She nodded, hoping it seemed like she actually knew how to help with horses. Her grandparents had one, but he stayed in the pasture most of the time and no one rode him.

"My fee comes when we win," he finished.

She noticed that he didn't say what it would be, and her heart thumped in a strange way, increasing when he said, "So, Miss Lily. Tell me about yourself."

———

HER COWBOY BILLIONAIRE BODYGUARD, featuring Beau Whittaker and Lily Everett, a big-time celebrity country singer, is ready for you to read! **It's now available in paperback.**

Keep scrolling to view series starters from three of my other series!

CORAL CANYON COWBOYS
ROMANCE SERIES

Visit stunning Wyoming for another family of cowboys... The Youngs! The series includes second chance romance, friends to lovers, family saga, Christian values, clean and sweet romance, single dads, equine therapy themes, police dog training, brotherly relationships, return to hometown, fish out of water, and country music stars!

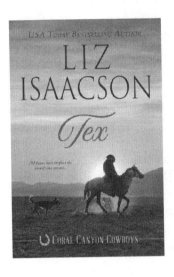

Tex (Book 1): He's back in town after a successful country music career. She owns a bordering farm to the family land he wants to buy...and she outbids him at the auction. **Can Tex and Abigail rekindle their old flame, or will the issue of land ownership come between them?**

BRUSH CREEK COWBOYS ROMANCE SERIES

Go up the canyon to Brush Creek Ranch, where a community of retired rodeo cowboys are looking for love...

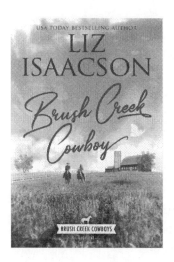

Brush Creek Cowboy (Book 1): Former rodeo champion and cowboy Walker Thompson trains horses at Brush Creek Horse Ranch, where he lives a simple life in his cabin with his ten-year-old son. A widower of six years, he's worked with Tess Wagner, a widow who came to Brush Creek to escape the turmoil of her life to give her seven-year-old son a slower pace of life. But Tess's breast cancer is back...

Walker will have to decide if he'd rather spend even a short time with Tess than not have her in his life at all. Tess wants to feel God's love and power, **but can she discover and accept God's will in order to find her happy ending?**

FULLER FAMILY IN BRUSH CREEK ROMANCE SERIES

Join the Fuller Family in Brush Creek for heartwarming and inspirational romance series set in a picturesque small town.

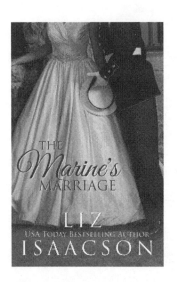

The Marine's Marriage: (Book 1): Tate Benson can't believe he's come to Nowhere, Utah, to fix up a house that hasn't been inhabited in years. But he has. Because he's retired from the Marines and looking to start a life as a police officer in small-town Brush Creek. Wren Fuller has her hands full most days running her family's company. When Tate calls and demands a maid for that morning, she decides to have the calls forwarded to her cell and go help him out. She didn't know he was moving in next door, and she's completely unprepared for his handsomeness, his kind heart, and his wounded soul. **Can Tate and Wren weather a relationship when they're also next-door neighbors?**

ABOUT LIZ

Liz Isaacson writes inspirational romance, usually set in Texas, or Wyoming, or anywhere else horses and cowboys exist. She lives in Utah, where she writes full-time, takes her two dogs to the park everyday, and eats a lot of veggies while writing. Find her on her website, along with all of her pen names, at feelgood-fictionbooks.com